Somebody Understands Me

by

Tushar Mehta

Tushar Mehta

Copyright © 2025

All Rights Reserved

ISBN:

Dedication

To my dearest mother,

Ilaben Girishbhai Mehta,

who left this world in 1993 but never left my heart.

Her peaceful nature, gentle soul, and unwavering spirit of humanity continue to guide me every single day. She was the embodiment of kindness—always calm, always helpful, and always full of quiet strength.

Though she is not here in the physical world, I feel her presence in everything I do. Her blessings walk with me, her values speak through me, and her love breathes life into every word I write.

This book is a reflection of what she stood for—**understanding, compassion, and emotional connection.**

She is my eternal source of strength, my silent guide, and the light behind *Somebody Understands Me.*

With endless love and gratitude,

—Tushar Mehta.

Acknowledgment

First and foremost, I bow in gratitude to the divine force that breathes life into every story, every emotion, and every connection. Without that source of inspiration, this book would never have found its way into the world.

Somebody Understands Me is more than a collection of stories—it is a piece of my soul. It took shape through moments of deep reflection, countless cups of chai, and the silent strength of those who believed in me when I questioned myself.

A masterpiece created after almost seven years of hard work and dedication, this book is a testament to patience, perseverance, and the power of heartfelt storytelling.

To my loving family and friends—thank you for walking this journey with me.

To my father—your positive approach, strength, and unwavering support have been the steady foundation of my life. I have witnessed you backing me up through every phase, doing everything possible for me and for our family. After your retirement, the way you embraced the double role of both a father and a mother has touched me deeply. Your quiet sacrifices and boundless love are etched in my heart forever. This book carries a part of your spirit in every word.

To my wife—your love has been my anchor. You have made countless sacrifices, especially in my absence while I travelled across countries for my career. You carried our world on your shoulders with grace and resilience. Thank you for holding everything together, for believing in me, and for giving me the space to pursue my dreams. This book would not exist without your silent courage and strength. To my son—your mental support has been my emotional fuel, and your readiness to become my financial wall when needed showed a maturity and love that touched me deeply. Your strength, belief, and generosity are etched in the heart of this book. I am so proud of the man you are.

To my daughter-in-law—your loving push, "Dad! You can do it," came at just the right time. Thank you for reminding me of my own strength when I forgot it. Your encouragement has meant the world to me.

To my dear sister—your role in my life has gone beyond just being a sibling. In the absence of our mother, you embraced me with her warmth, her care, and her nurturing spirit. Your love has been my emotional foundation.

To all my cousins—thank you for being my cheerleaders and for your consistent encouragement, love, and belief in this dream of mine. Your bond means more than words can express. To my close friends—how can I ever forget you? Your names are engraved in my heart. Your belief in me, your patience through my quiet phases, and your joy in my little victories have all helped carry me here.

To my incredible community on Facebook, Instagram, and YouTube—more than 10,000 of you have followed, supported, and encouraged my journey through *Happinez Within*. Your likes, shares, comments, and heartfelt messages reminded me that the stories I share matter. Thank you for being my extended family and for standing by me, story after story.

To my readers and kindred spirits—you reminded me that stories heal, that words connect, and that someone always understands.

To my publisher, proofreaders, and the design team—thank you for bringing professionalism, creativity, and care into every stage of this book's creation. Your dedication turned this manuscript into a meaningful, polished piece of work. My special gratitude goes to those who read early drafts, offered thoughtful reviews, and guided me with honest feedback throughout my writing journey. You helped shape these stories into what they are today.

A special thank you to the people who opened up their hearts and shared their real-life emotions and experiences with me—you trusted me with your truths, and this book stands as a tribute to your courage.

Lastly, to every soul who has ever longed to be understood—you are not alone. This book is for you.

With love and deep gratitude,

Tushar.

Table of Contents

About the Author

A Silent Revolution in Human Connection: The Unfinished Masterpiece of Tushar Mehta

In a world that often seems too busy to pause and listen, a quiet yet powerful movement is unfolding—spearheaded by none other than hard-core sales professional Tushar Mehta. Through his upcoming book, *Somebody Understands Me*, Tushar is nurturing not just minds but souls.

Though the book is still in the making, its short stories—shared across platforms like Facebook, Instagram, and YouTube—are already touching hearts. The response has been nothing short of phenomenal. People are resonating deeply with the emotional fabric of each narrative, finding fragments of their own lives reflected within the stories.

Somebody Understands Me is not merely a book; it's a journey. A collection of short stories intricately woven with one central theme—understanding. The title itself raises a poignant question: *Is there truly someone who understands me?* This yearning, this silent cry for connection, is something almost all of us carry.

Each story in the collection explores the raw, unspoken layers of human relationships. Whether it's the quiet tension between a husband and wife, the fragile bond between a parent and child, the vulnerability in a romantic relationship, or the often-overlooked emotions within professional dynamics—these tales hold up a mirror to everyday life.

In a world clouded by stress and endless expectations, understanding each other has become an increasingly rare art. Misunderstandings grow like weeds in the garden of our relationships, choking the possibility of deeper connection. Tushar's stories aim to heal—to offer not just perspective but empathy. Through his storytelling, he aspires to create moments of pause, reflection, and, ultimately, reconciliation.

A few of these emotionally charged stories have already been published on his Facebook page, *Happinez Within*, and have garnered immense appreciation. The remaining stories will be gradually released across his social media platforms.

Tushar Mehta's intention is crystal clear—to help people bridge emotional gaps and rediscover the power of genuine human understanding. If you are someone who cherishes stories that stir the heart and soul, who seeks clarity in chaos, or simply wants to feel seen, heard, and understood—follow *Happinez Within.* Because sometimes, all we need is to know that *somebody understands us.*

Preface

Somebody Understands Me
From the Window of the Heart
By Tushar Mehta

Dear Reader,

Nowadays, screen time has taken over most of our lives, often leaving us feeling more alone than ever.

The question is—how can we convert screen time into quality time?

While screen time is essential in today's world, developing the habit of mindful, meaningful screen usage can lead us toward more peace and happiness. Reading books and engaging with good literature has almost vanished from our routines. Yet, quality reading is not a luxury—it's a necessity. It's about consciously deciding to shift our patterns and create space for stillness and reflection.

This book is intended for all generations—from teenagers to retired individuals. It aims to help readers of every age reframe their thinking and develop a deeper attitude of understanding, something that feels increasingly rare in our fast-paced world.

If you're a teenager, this book may help you redesign your upcoming life. If you're in midlife, it can bring more clarity and bliss into your daily journey. And if you're retired, it can add depth and meaning to your golden years. The only essential step is this: start reading.

Before you dive into these pages, I gently invite you to take a moment—to breathe, to feel, and to read not just with your eyes but with your heart.

If you enjoy reflections on life, heartfelt stories, and meaningful poetry, I'd love to welcome you into my creative world. You can find more of my work on Facebook, Instagram, and YouTube under *Happinez Within*—safe spaces where stories meet souls, just like the ones you'll find in this book.

"Somebody Understands Me" is more than just a title.

It's the culmination of nearly seven years of deep listening, observing, writing, and healing. This journey wasn't easy. I met people from all walks of life, listened to their stories, studied the nuances of human behaviour, and reflected on the emotional patterns that connect us all.

Each story in this book is rooted in real emotions, shaped by authentic experiences, and designed to offer moments of recognition, healing, and hope.

Haven't we all felt it at different moments in our lives?

The ache of not being understood.

The silent hope that someone—just one person—might see us clearly, without the need for explanation.

How often have we thought, *"No one understands me...?"*

And yet, at that very moment, someone close to us might be thinking the same.

In a world full of speed and noise, misunderstandings are natural. A missed moment of empathy, a tiny gap in expectation—and suddenly, we're distant not just from others but from ourselves.

Psychologists refer to this deep desire as Self-Verification Theory—our need to be seen in alignment with how we see ourselves. When others respond in ways that don't reflect our inner truth, it creates a painful disconnect. And over time, we may internalize the belief: *"No one understands me."*

This belief can quietly reshape our relationships. It can lead to withdrawal, conflict, or a quiet sense of loneliness. But it doesn't have to.

This book is a collection of gentle, thoughtful stories—born from everyday moments, layered with emotional insight. You may find echoes of your own life in them: unspoken thoughts, familiar feelings, quiet realizations.

Each story invites reflection:

What does it truly mean to be understood?

Do I offer others the same understanding I seek?

Am I expressing myself with compassion—or only with expectation?

Dear reader,

Somebody Understands Me is not just a book.

It's a mirror.

A companion.

A quiet voice whispering, *"You are not alone."*

Let these stories comfort you, stir you, and remind you:

You are worthy of being understood. And of understanding others.

Disclaimer:
All characters, names, and incidents in this book are fictional. Any resemblance to real persons, living or deceased, is purely coincidental. These stories are intended to inspire, comfort, and provoke thought— not to hurt or offend any individual or belief.

With warmth,

Tushar Mehta.

From the Window of the Heart – Somebody Understands Me

📌 Follow me on Facebook, Instagram & YouTube: Happinez Within

Who should understand whom?

How wonderful it would be if life flowed peacefully like the stream of a river, gentle, like calm, cool water, flowing easily with the breeze. The way the river flows without any obstruction, one would expect the years of one's life to pass by in the same peaceful manner, right?

It's natural to have this expectation, isn't it? But when we think about the two banks of the river, one thing becomes clear – the two banks of the river run alongside each other but can never meet. Some relationships in life are like the two banks of the river. They can run alongside each other, but they can never meet.

You can see such banks in every home these days. I'm not talking about relationships between husband and wife or lovers, but rather the relationship between parents and children.

At first glance, you might think that this is about the generational gap, which is quite common. But no, this is not about the generational gap. Just think about it for a moment – what if the two banks of the river actually meet? The flow of the river would stop, right? Similarly, as parents, we often wish that our lives, like the flow of a river, run smoothly with our children, but on the other hand, we also wish for both banks to stay together. That is, not just physically, but mentally too – that the children adopt the mindset of their parents. This means the children should think the way their parents think and follow their way of life. But tell me, how is this even possible?

Pallavi and Rajesh are on one bank of the river, and their two children, Kartavya and Nisha, are on the other bank.

Kartavya and Nisha were raised with the same love and affection, just as children are raised in most of our homes. Soon, it was time for college, and like most children, Kartavya and Nisha also dreamed of going abroad for higher education to build their best careers.

It is quite natural for parents to plan the finances for their children's higher education and weddings. Rajesh and Pallavi had already planned for this situation.

This is the true dignity of Indian culture. Let me share an experience I had in America. As part of my daily routine, I went for my evening walk. Every day, I would see a young man, born and raised in America, probably 19-20 years old, who would greet me with a "Hi." Gradually, our acquaintance grew, and one day, I casually asked him, "Where do you live?" His response took me aback. He casually said, "Uncle, I live nearby with my friends."

Naturally, I asked, "Don't your parents live here in America? Are they in India?" He laughed and said, "No, my parents live here in America, too, just two miles away from my place." This response piqued my curiosity, so I asked, "Why don't you live with them?"

His answer surprised me. He said, "Uncle, actually, the rent my father asks from me is something I can't afford." And this is a true story. I'm not criticizing American culture, but simply pointing out the difference between Indian culture and here. In America, when a child turns 16,

they are expected to take responsibility for themselves. But in India, parents usually bear the responsibility for their children until they finish their higher education. Some children may even wonder what the big deal is about their parents' sacrifices. But this is not a sacrifice; it is a commitment that Indian parents fulfill without being asked.

Now, let's get back to the matter at hand. Pallavi, Rajesh, Kartavya, and Nisha decided together that Kartavya would go to America for higher studies this year, and Nisha would go two years later. The arrow shot from the bow of time passed quickly, and soon, Kartavya and Nisha were both in America for their studies. And thus began the series of "Who will understand whom?"

Who should understand whom? Parents understanding children, or children understanding their parents? This thought emerged from the expectations. Small, little expectations grew so much that before we realized it, the children seemed to be drifting away from their parents.

Initially, after Kartavya and Nisha arrived in America, they would talk every day via WhatsApp – either through calls or messages. Naturally, they felt lonely, but they didn't want their parents, Rajesh and Pallavi, to feel lonely either. Slowly, the two kids got busy with their studies and also started working part-time jobs so that they wouldn't add to their parent's financial burden. They still made an effort to stay in touch once a day, but over time, they started to forget. Rajesh and Pallavi began to complain, "What happened? Are you so busy that you can't spare even a minute to call?" At first, they would say it calmly, but eventually, it turned into frustration. The tone of their calls changed, and instead of love, there was annoyance in their voice.

Whenever the children called, the parents' first words were, "Oh, what's the matter? You finally found time to call today?" Thus began the growing distance between parents and children.

Who should understand whom? Should parents understand their children, or should children understand their parents? We immediately think, "What's the big deal? Both sides just need to understand each other a little." But in reality, it's not that easy. Parents think, "We raised them, sacrificed so much for them, and yet they don't seem to understand." But do they ever stop to think that the reason we are saying this is because we care?

On the other hand, children become so confused that they don't understand why their parents seem so upset. It seems like they've forgotten that the flow of the river cannot be stopped. It only works when the river flows freely, just like the love and understanding in a relationship.

Parents give their children the physical freedom to go out into the world, but mentally, they never let go. Children are constantly worried that if they don't call or message, their parents will be upset. What was once a loving call is now a call driven by fear.

Parents don't realize that holding on too tightly leads to unnecessary pressure. They forget that relationships need space to grow. When we try to stop the river's flow, it stagnates, and when water stagnates, it starts to stink. Similarly, in relationships, if we don't give space, they will start to feel suffocating and unpleasant.

I recall an experience from a few years ago. At the age of 22 or 23, I developed a passion for keeping a parrot. I brought a costly parrot in a cage and took great care of it. I fed it fruits and chilies and thought how lucky it was to have such a caring owner. After a few months, I noticed that the parrot seemed inactive, and something made me feel that it had become depressed.

One day, I decided to free it. I opened the cage, expecting it to fly away and never return. But after two or three days, I heard the parrot's voice again. It had a red thread tied to its leg, so I recognized it. I gave it food, and it happily ate and then flew away. After a few days, it came back again, and this continued for years.

What is the moral of this story? I gave the parrot freedom, and it came back willingly every day. Similarly, in every relationship, space is crucial.

A few years later, Kartavya and Nisha returned to India after completing their studies. Both wanted to settle in America. They were sure their parents would support them and allow them to stay there. The parents were surprised when the children shared this decision, and after some discussion, they all agreed that Kartavya and Nisha would stay in America.

However, even at the end of the discussion, the children seemed a little worried and hesitant. Rajesh immediately understood and asked them, "What's wrong? Why do you look worried?"

Nisha gently replied, "We're both upset. For the past few months, when we talk, the conversations have become more tense rather than joyful. We know we haven't been calling or messaging as regularly, and we feel that both of you are upset with us. You both often scold us without understanding the reason. We don't want to tell you everything because we want to take care of our expenses, and that's why we're working two part-time jobs. But when we call, we just want to talk peacefully, but now we feel pressured. We even go a week without talking to each other sometimes."

At that moment, both Rajesh and Pallavi understood. They had never realized that their constant expectation of calls and messages had put emotional pressure on their children. Rajesh said, "We didn't realize that our constant need for contact was causing you stress. We thought we were just checking in, but we see now that it was putting unnecessary pressure on you."

After a long and open discussion, everyone felt much lighter. Pallavi thought to herself that before her children were born, she was much more carefree. She wondered whether her love for her parents had changed.

This story is not just about children going abroad. Similar struggles arise even in homes where children stay with their parents. When children go out, and there is no phone call or message, it creates an emotional distance.

The way to overcome this situation is simple: Parents should not impose pressure on children to give a minute-by-minute account of their lives. Children should understand that their parents just want a small connection to feel reassured.

If both sides develop understanding and patience, there will come a time when no one has to say, "Who will understand me?" Both parents and children will trust each other, give each other space, and strengthen their bond.

So, when you are in a relationship, whether with your children or parents, understand this simple principle – "Let them go with love, and they will come back willingly." Let the river flow freely without trying to control it. This is the essence of love and understanding.

Anything Will Do: A Story of Love, Misunderstandings, and Understanding

Take something as simple as a question often asked at home:

"What should I cook today?" A reply like *"Anything will do"* might seem harmless. But it can feel like an unintentional dismissal of effort, a lack of interest. Because behind that question is often a desire to be seen, to be included, to be appreciated.

In our office, when we work on a project, we often seek advice or suggestions from colleagues or supervisors. But what if, when you ask, *"What should we do next in this project?"* the response you get is, *"Anything will do."* How do you proceed with clarity?

Now, imagine you run a business, and you seek financial advice from your chartered accountant. You ask, *"How should I record this entry?"* and he replies, *"Anything will do."* Would that resolve your confusion—or add to it?

The phrase *"Anything will do"* is often casually tossed around. But in relationships—especially in marriages—it can carry hidden landmines. It's like handing someone a firecracker and pretending it's a flower. The explosion might not be immediate, but it's inevitable.

Tarun and Ketki were once the couple everyone admired.

They were madly in love. Friends turned soulmates, bound not just by affection but deep admiration. Their love marriage was filled with warmth, silly surprises, and whispered late-night dreams.

Ketki, though not an expert in cooking, made it her mission to learn Tarun's favourite dishes. From burnt chapatis to delicious misal pav, she went through every cooking tutorial she could find online. Tarun adored her efforts. He'd kiss her forehead and say, *"Even if you give me burnt rice, I'll still eat it with love."

But as the honeymoon period of marriage settled into routine life, a new reality began to emerge—one they hadn't fully noticed as friends or lovers. They realized that while their hearts were deeply connected, their personalities were strikingly different. Tarun was a morning person who loved the structure, while Ketki found her creativity blooming after midnight. He enjoyed watching thrillers; she preferred emotional dramas. His idea of a relaxing Sunday was cricket and chai; hers was reading a book in silence with soft music.

As friends, they had always seen the exciting side of each other—their jokes, their dreams, their chemistry. But marriage brought the full picture. Tarun didn't quite understand Ketki's obsession with organizing kitchen drawers, and Ketki found Tarun's love for high-end gadgets a bit excessive. They began to feel like they were walking on parallel roads—close but not meeting.

The misunderstandings began to pile up. A forgotten anniversary. A sarcastic comment said in frustration. A misinterpreted silence. One evening, Ketki waited with dinner ready for two hours, only to find out Tarun had eaten outside with colleagues. No message. No call. Just a casual "I was busy."

Ketki started feeling invisible. Her excitement to share her day dimmed. Her voice got softer. Her smiles grew fewer.

Tarun, on the other hand, began feeling constantly judged. He believed he was working hard to provide, yet felt like no matter what he did, it wasn't enough. He started coming home late intentionally, just to avoid more arguments.

Nights that once ended in cuddles and whispered dreams now ended in cold shoulders and turning away.

They fought over toothpaste tubes, laundry, and TV remotes. But deep down, it wasn't about these things. It was about the unspoken pain. The love that once brought them together now sat quietly in a corner, suffocating under egos and misunderstandings.

It reached a point where even their closest friends noticed. They stopped going out. Photos stopped being posted. Conversations turned to chores. Smiles became forced. And laughter? Almost extinct.

There were small misunderstandings. When Ketki spent hours planning a cozy indoor date, Tarun would wish they had gone out instead. When Tarun spent a weekend watching cricket non-stop, Ketki felt ignored. The things that once felt cute and tolerable started becoming frustrating. They both began to wonder silently— *"Were we too different?"*

As time passed, screen time became the silent villain in their story. Even when they sat on the same couch, their eyes remained fixed on phones, laptops, or tablets. Tarun would scroll through emails or social media while Ketki watched cooking videos or read online. Human touch began fading—not physically, but emotionally. The comfort of looking into each other's eyes, sharing smiles, or simple thoughts began to disappear. Instead of talking about their days, they consumed content in isolation. The blue glow of the screen replaced the warmth of connection. Their world became quieter—not with peace, but with emotional distance. That warmth, the one that once lingered in late-night talks and stolen kisses, was now replaced by virtual noise and digital silence.

But what saved their love was not similarity—it was their growing attitude of understanding. Instead of resisting each other's differences, they slowly began to embrace them. Tarun started sitting beside Ketki while she read, simply holding her hand and enjoying the silence. Ketki, though never a sports fan, began watching cricket highlights with him—just to be part of his world. He gifted her a personalized bookshelf; she surprised him with a digital subscription to his favourite tech magazine.

They didn't change for each other. They grew with each other.

That shift—from reacting to understanding—changed everything. Instead of competing over whose way was right, they began to celebrate how their different worlds added colour to their shared life. And in that acceptance, they found not just peace but lasting joy.

Tarun also loved buying expensive, branded gifts for Ketki on special occasions.

As time passed, their busy careers took priority. The thoughtful gestures faded, and small arguments turned into big fights. One day, on Valentine's Day, Ketki excitedly asked Tarun, *"What should I cook tonight?"* She wanted to prepare a candlelight dinner as a surprise.

But Tarun, busy on his laptop, casually responded, *"Anything will do. Why do you ask the same thing every day? You're a woman—you should know what to cook!"*

Ketki was heartbroken. The excitement of Valentine's Day vanished instantly. She softly replied, *"My career is my dream, but my home is my responsibility. I never ignored my duties."*

But Tarun snapped back, *"You're not the only woman managing both career and home. Millions do it! You're not doing a Favour!"*

Ketki was speechless. She wasn't asking for appreciation—just some involvement, a little interest from her husband. She thought to herself, *"I just wanted him to help me decide. I wanted him to care, not treat it as a duty."*

Later that night, Tarun stormed out of the house in anger while Ketki cried herself to sleep.

When Tarun returned home, he noticed an envelope on the bedside table. Curious, he opened it and was stunned—it was a medical report confirming Ketki's pregnancy, along with a greeting card that said, *"Congratulations, you're going to be a father!"*

Tears filled Tarun's eyes. He felt a mix of happiness and guilt. Ketki had planned to surprise him with this news during their romantic dinner, and instead, he had ruined the evening with his careless words.

For the next week, they barely spoke. Then, on Ketki's birthday, something unexpected happened. She woke up to find an envelope beside her bed. It read, *"I'm sorry."*

Surprised, she looked around for Tarun and found him in the kitchen, struggling to cook something.

Shocked, she asked, *"What are you doing?"*

Scratching his head, Tarun smiled awkwardly, *"Trying to cook something for you... but I'm confused. Can you tell me what to make?"*

Ketki, still teasing him, replied, *"Anything will do."* And they both burst into laughter.

Ketki then opened the envelope. Inside was a weekly meal plan with Tarun's list of what to cook each day. He also took responsibility for buying the groceries. Most importantly, every Sunday, they would cook together!

Ketki's eyes filled with happy tears. This was not about cooking—it was about feeling valued, supported, and loved.

Their life began to change—not with one big moment, but with hundreds of small ones.

Tarun made time every evening to talk—not about tasks or plans, but about feelings. He realized Ketki never needed grand gifts. She needed his attention, his involvement. Just someone who'd ask, *"How was your day?"* and mean it.

Ketki, too, began to see how stressed Tarun was. The pressure at work, the constant expectations, the silent battles he never spoke about. She started asking, *"Want to talk about your day?"* She left sticky notes on his laptop with lines like: *"You're doing great."* or *"One day at a time, love."*

They started evening walks. No phones. Just hands held tightly.

Cooking together became a ritual. They laughed, teased, fought over too much salt, and fed each other like newlyweds. The kitchen became their haven. And love—once buried under work and fatigue—returned in every stir, every slice, every shared plate.

It's not just about cooking. This need for understanding exists in every little corner of daily life—whether it's sharing a household chore, managing expenses, or simply deciding how to spend a Sunday. For Tarun and Ketki, it wasn't just the food question that created distance. Slowly, they started misreading each other's silences.

When Ketki stayed late at work, Tarun assumed she was losing interest in home life. When Tarun sat glued to his phone or laptop, Ketki felt invisible, like she didn't matter anymore. They began to withdraw, not out of lack of love but due to unspoken disappointments. Screen time started replacing quality time. Even when they were physically together, their eyes were on different screens—scrolling endlessly while the warmth between them faded.

The emotional distance didn't erupt overnight; it quietly grew from all the moments they stopped noticing each other's needs. A shared coffee went cold on the table. A smile went unseen. A sigh went unheard. And before they knew it, they were sitting next to each other, yet living worlds apart.

But love, when nurtured with attention, has the power to bring people back. All it takes is one moment of awareness, one step closer, one hand reaching out and saying, *"I'm here, I see you."*

This story isn't just about food. It's about understanding.

When a woman asks, *"What should I cook?"*
She's not asking for a recipe. She's seeking inclusion.
When a man stays quiet, it's not always ignorance.
Sometimes, it's exhaustion.

We all want to be heard, seen, and valued—not just as spouses but as individuals with emotions and dreams.

So, the next time someone asks something as simple as, *"What should I cook today?"* Don't say, *"Anything will do."* Say, *"Let's figure it out together."*

Because the strongest marriages aren't built on grand gestures; they're built on tiny acts of understanding, patience, and shared silence.

Let's not just live with each other.
Let's live *for* each other.

Somebody Understands Me

A Recipe Called Love *(Poem)*

In kitchens warm and hearts awake,
A question stirs, a bond to make.
"What should I cook?" she softly said—
Not for a dish, but love instead.

He glanced up once, then looked away,
"Anything will do," he let slip that day.
But words have weight, and silence speaks,
Of tired hearts and wounded weeks.

Two souls who once danced in sync,
Now paused on edge, afraid to blink.
Yet love's not lost—it only hides,
In whispered thoughts and shifting tides.

He learns to see, she learns to bend,
They meet halfway; they start to mend.
From gadgets laid to books, she'd share,
From cricket scores to songs of care.

They stir and simmer, spice and smile,
And cook together once in a while.
The secret's not in what you do—
But showing up and seeing through.

So hold that hand, reply with grace,
Look beyond the daily race.
For love is built in small replies,
In thoughtful nods and softened sighs.

Not in the stars, not far above—
But in a kitchen, with a recipe called Love.

Preksha – Finally, Somebody Understood Me

(A Journey of a Young, Beautiful, and Vibrant Married Woman to Find True Happiness)

Preksha was a young, beautiful, and lively woman. Her eyes sparkled with dreams, and her heart beat with joy. Born in 1995 in a small but culturally rich town in Gujarat, she had been cheerful and carefree from childhood. She loved going out with her friends, spending hours chatting in malls and cafés, and watching the latest Bollywood movies. The excitement of spontaneous plans with friends, going to gardens or eateries, and spending time in fun-filled activities were things she truly enjoyed. She didn't just live life; she embraced every corner of it, coloring her world in her own shades and making others paint with her colors.

Preksha always dreamed of an independent life. She wanted to live on her own terms, build a professional career, and find a partner who would not just be a husband but someone who would care for her, understand her, and stand by her as a friend. However, at the age of 22, her parents arranged her marriage with Piyush against her wishes. Piyush, who was 25 years old, came from a happy and well-cultured family. Before Preksha could even get to know him, the pressure from her family made her agree to the marriage.

Even on her wedding day, as she stepped into the wedding mandap, she felt an unfamiliar emptiness. She had an unspoken fear: Will my life partner ever understand me?

After the wedding, Preksha's life fell into a routine. The first five to seven years passed in adjusting to the new phase. Piyush was a good man, a responsible husband, and a loving family member, but he could never understand Preksha's heart. For him, marriage was merely a social responsibility, not love. Due to the age difference, Piyush often behaved as if he were her elder, forgetting that Preksha was also his friend. He misunderstood her every emotion and stayed busy with his own work. To him, Preksha was the only one who managed the home and looked after his parents and relatives. He never realized that Preksha had her own desires, likes, and dislikes.

In seven years, Preksha became a mother of three. Motherhood brought her some joy, and she never held back in raising her children well. Yet, the emptiness caused by the lack of love and communication could not be filled. She sometimes felt that her relationship with Piyush was confined to duties and everyday tasks. Her life revolved around satisfying her family during the day and Piyush in the night. While she gave her children the best upbringing and won everyone's hearts at home, what about her own heart? No one seemed to think about it.

At 33, she was merely existing, not truly living.

One day, while strolling through Facebook on a neighbor's phone, she found herself in a new world—a world where people shared their thoughts, posted photos, and reconnected with old friends. This was magical for Preksha! She created her own Facebook account, became active on Instagram, and WhatsApp became her life partner. In just a few days, she started reconnecting with school friends, college crushes, and even strangers. The attention and admiration she never received from Piyush she started to get from the virtual world. Lost in a world of brand-new clothes, admiration, and glamour, she began to feel like a social media celebrity.

In an attempt to escape loneliness and the emotional warmth she lacked from Piyush, she started chatting with numerous people. Some promised her false love, while others approached her purely for physical attraction. In the end, they all treated her as a beautiful, needy woman and used her emotions. True to her nature, she tried to please everyone and remained positive. They admired her appearance, but ultimately, all they wanted was her body.

Among all this, she met a younger man who often came to the gym where she worked out. He was strong, fair, and had large, captivating eyes. A friendship blossomed between them, and it seemed like they were partners in both happiness and sorrow. But destiny didn't allow this bond to flourish. Due to the age gap or perhaps a decline in physical attraction, the young man soon fell in love with a girl of his own age and started making excuses to avoid Preksha. He even threatened to post Preksha's private photos on social media, as he was getting bored of her.

That's when Preksha realized that everyone was using her. Even her close friends were emotionally exploiting her. She broke down, realizing that she had been looking for love in the wrong places.

Hours spent on social media, talking on the phone, and saving other people's emotions became her daily routine. Preksha took a moment to reflect on her past, thinking about what she had lost and what she had gained. She realized that the most important relationship for a woman is not with an external person but with herself.

She made a new decision—she would now focus on self-improvement rather than regret. She would laugh again, live again, and make an attempt to live life to the fullest. She decided to join dance classes, something she had loved in her childhood but had forgotten after marriage.

Her children became her whole world. She started participating in their school events and spending quality time with them. The atmosphere at home changed. Now, Preksha didn't need any external emotional support. She had found the world she had once dreamed of. Witnessing this transformation, Piyush was left astonished.

One day, after a dance competition, when Preksha came down from the stage, Piyush and their children applauded her—seeing that, tears of joy welled up in her eyes once again.

Piyush came to her, smiled gently, and said, "Preksha, you are not just my wife; you are the most beautiful truth of my life. You've come back... I've got my children's laughing, playful mother back."

Piyush realized that in everything Preksha had done, he, too, was at fault. Preksha had always been the one to keep the family together, and for Piyush, she was everything. He acknowledged that he had never tried to live life from Preksha's perspective and had always had excuses.

Preksha didn't say anything, just gazed into Piyush's eyes. For the first time, she felt a sweet vibration in their relationship. It might not have been as romantic as she had once dreamed, but there was a hidden meaning in those words, which was invaluable to her.

Her children hugged her and asked, "Mom, will you always be this happy now?"

With a soft reply, Preksha said, "Yes, my children, always!"

Seeing her happy, Piyush decided that he would never let her feel alone again. He made up his mind that a wife is not just a homemaker but a partner and a companion, and he would keep her happy as a true-life partner.

Three years later, Preksha opened an online music academy. She found her new identity, and Piyush helped her set everything up online. He started taking an active interest in her dance classes and their work together. Perhaps what Preksha truly needed was attention, care, and friendship. Piyush was now truly happy about this and felt a change in his life, which had a positive impact on his work. That year, Piyush received the Best Employee of the Year award.

Preksha's life started afresh.

Friends woke up from where they had once dreamed. The past was just a dream, and a new beginning is the true key to a successful life. Preksha had found hers. Now, it's our turn.

This story is a reminder that happiness and fulfillment come from self-acceptance, love, and strong relationships with those who truly care.

A Newly Married Couple – How Love Survived the Storm of Misunderstanding

Pranav and Pankti had dreamt of a perfect life together. After marriage, they imagined a happy, peaceful, and romantic life. Their honeymoon memories were still fresh—the moments spent on the beach and the promises made under the stars.

In the early days of their marriage, their home was filled with laughter and love. Pranav, a software engineer, mostly worked from home, while Pankti, a writer, loved spending time creating stories. They cooked together, watched movies, and had long conversations at night. Sunday mornings were for pancakes and music, and evenings often ended with soft jazz, scented candles, and deep talks about their dreams.

They would surprise each other with little notes, plan spontaneous picnics in the park, and even slow dance in the living room. Their joy was pure, effortless, and brimming with hope. Friends admired their bond, calling them the perfect couple. They felt like nothing could come between them.

However, gradually, a new habit began eating into their togetherness—the excessive use of mobile phones. What once was a dinner filled with conversations and laughter now had long silences interrupted by scrolling. Even their bedtime talks were replaced by screen time. Instead of sharing thoughts, they began sharing memes. Instead of holding hands, they held their phones.

They were in the same room but miles apart.

The mobile screen slowly became a wall. Pankti noticed Pranav's constant notifications and unread messages taking priority over her voice. Pranav, on the other hand, felt ignored when Pankti immersed herself in replying to social media comments rather than replying to his questions.

What once felt like a sanctuary now felt like a house filled with unspoken words. They stopped noticing the little things that once brought them closer. A missed hug, an overlooked compliment, a forgotten dinner—small things that used to matter became normal.

Happiness quietly slipped out, replaced by silent expectations and unshared burdens. Misunderstandings began to sprout from assumptions, and those assumptions hardened into emotional distance.

One day, a woman named Priyanka entered Pranav's life. She was managing a new project in his office. Priyanka was understanding and always appreciated Pranav's work. He started feeling that Priyanka understood him better than Pankti, while the emotional distance between him and Pankti kept growing.

One evening, Pankti asked, "Pranav, don't you feel that we have changed?"

Pranav looked up and replied, "What has changed?"

"We're not the same as before. We don't laugh together, talk like we used to, or spend quality time anymore."

Pranav sighed, "Pankti, work pressure is too much. And you are always busy with your writing. Maybe it's just a phase."

But Pankti was not satisfied with this answer. She felt hurt by the lack of communication, the growing distance, and the decreasing warmth in their relationship. Over time, Pranav became more distant, and Pankti started feeling lonely.

One evening, Pankti asked, "Pranav, are you truly happy?"

Pranav sighed and replied, "I don't know, Pankti. Something is missing."

Pankti calmly responded, "Should we try to find what's missing?"

A New Beginning – Pankti's Experiment

One day, Pankti started reading a book called Ikigai. It talked about ten simple principles to make life happy and stress-free. She decided to follow these principles to save their marriage:

1. Communicate and Listen – Open-hearted conversations are necessary.

2. Appreciate Each Other – Recognize and praise each other despite the daily rush.

3. Spend Time Together – Even a little time together daily strengthens the bond.

4.	Create Memories – Find happiness in small things and make special moments.

5.	Support and Empathize – Understand each other's struggles and emotions.

6.	Let Go of Ego and Anger – Avoid unnecessary arguments and express expectations in a healthy way.

7.	Keep Romance Alive – Small gestures and special moments keep love fresh.

8.	Personal Growth – Self-improvement brings new energy to relationships.

9.	Trust and Respect – Honour each other's emotions and boundaries.

10.	Enjoy Life Together – Marriage is not just a responsibility; it's a beautiful journey.

Together, they reflected on what went wrong in their relationship.

Reasons for Their Growing Distance

1.	Lack of Time – In the beginning, they spent a lot of time together, but work pressure and career commitments slowly pulled them apart.

2.	Poor Communication – Their deep conversations turned into just discussing responsibilities. The lack of emotional discussions made them feel lonely.

3.	Different Expectations – Pranav felt that Pankti didn't understand his work pressure, while Pankti felt that Pranav was becoming indifferent to her feelings.

4.	Unwanted Stress – Small issues turned into big arguments, adding to the tension.

5.	Imbalance in Effort – When one person keeps giving while the other only takes, the relationship becomes strained. Pankti felt that she was putting in all the effort while Pranav was not responding.

6.	Overuse of Mobile Phones – Technology started replacing intimacy. Their screen time replaced their quality time, and virtual distractions slowly ate away at their emotional connection.

How Their Problems Escalated

• Growing Frustration – Even though they were together, they felt emotionally distant.

• Silence and Avoidance – Pranav started staying silent to avoid conflicts, which made Pankti even more upset.

• Attraction to an Outside Relationship – When someone feels unfulfilled in a relationship, they might get attracted to someone else. For Pranav, Priyanka seemed to be a better companion.

All of these issues led to cracks in their once-loving relationship.

Pranav's Realization and Effort

When Pranav heard about the Ikigai principles, he was hesitant at first, but Pankti's words made him think. He remembered something he had read before, similar to Ikegai's rules.

It felt like he had found the key to reviving their marriage. He realized that every relationship faces ups and downs, but if things feel dull and lifeless, effort is needed to bring back happiness.

Pranav took a piece of paper and listed a few important points:

1.   Open Communication – Talk openly about feelings, worries, and expectations. Honest conversations reduce misunderstandings.

2.   Give Time – Love and understanding don't grow automatically; they require time. Plan vacations and dinner dates, or simply be present for each other.

3.   Trust and Commitment – Forget past mistakes and move forward with new energy. Trust strengthens love.

4.   Appreciation and Gratitude – Show small gestures of love and thankfulness. This keeps relationships fresh and meaningful.

5.   Bring Excitement – Take interest in each other's hobbies, learn new things together, and try fun activities to add new energy to the relationship.

6.   Forgiveness and Understanding – Let go of past mistakes and be willing to understand each other's perspectives.

A Fresh Start

Slowly, Pranav and Pankti started following these principles. They talked more, spent time together, and found joy in small moments.

Pranav finally realized that love requires constant effort. He thought about his connection with Priyanka and understood that it was just an illusion. Priyanka could never replace what he had with Pankti.

One day, Pranav sat down with Pankti and had an open conversation. Pankti also shared that love needs continuous effort to make the other person feel valued.

They rediscovered each other, and this time, they promised never to let go.

The Power of Deep Understanding

Understanding isn't just about listening to words—it's about sensing the silence behind them. Pankti began to notice not only what Pranav said but what he *didn't* say. His tired eyes after long meetings. His silence at dinner. His subtle sighs when he thought she wasn't looking.

And Pranav began to see beyond Pankti's composed smile. He saw her waiting by the window, notebook closed, dinner gone cold. He began to realize that her writing wasn't a distraction—it was a lonely companion she turned to when he became unavailable.

They both understood something powerful—that love alone wasn't enough. It needed presence. Awareness. Willingness.

They stopped trying to win arguments. Instead, they started asking, "What hurt you?" They stopped counting who did more. Instead, they asked, "How can I support you better?"

When Pankti had a stressful day, Pranav would quietly make her favourite tea and sit beside her, saying nothing, just offering presence.

When Pranav looked drained after work, Pankti would gently place her hand on his shoulder—not to advise, not to question, but to say, "I see you. I'm here."

Understanding became their love language.

They learned that sometimes the most important words are unspoken—offered in eye contact, in shared silence, in simply choosing not to walk away.

They made space for each other's individuality without letting it become a barrier. They stopped trying to fix each other and instead started *holding space* for each other's flaws and fears.

They began to rebuild—not a perfect marriage, but a strong one.

The Gift of Choosing Each Other Again

Every morning was a quiet promise. Not that they'd never fight. Not that things would always be perfect. But that they'd try. Again and again.

They learned to say, *"I'm sorry,"* without ego. To say, *"I need you,"* without fear. To say, *"I love you,"* even when things weren't easy.

And in this daily choice to understand rather than assume, to empathize rather than judge—they found peace.

Their love became mature. Rooted. Steady. No longer just passion—but purpose. No longer just romance—but respect.

In the End...

Now, neither Pranav nor Pankti ever says, "You don't understand me."

Because they've learned to listen even when it's hard, to stay even when it's uncomfortable, and to grow—together, not apart.

Their love didn't just survive misunderstanding—it blossomed because of it.

Because sometimes, the storm doesn't destroy—it clears the air, deepens the roots, and teaches us how to truly love.

Garb Sanskar: The First Embrace

Mira and Aarav had always shared something beautiful—a bond that began as a friendship and blossomed into a quiet, steady love. When they got married, it wasn't just the beginning of a new life together; it was the deepening of something already sacred. They were partners in every sense—laughing at midnight jokes, holding each other through work stress, exploring new cities, and finding joy in the ordinary.

Both were software engineers living in a fast-paced world, but they found their calm in yoga. It wasn't just exercise—it became a ritual. A daily offering of breath, balance, and stillness that connected them to something greater than themselves.

One morning, Mira awoke with a strange sensation—a mix of fatigue and unfamiliar restlessness. A quick visit to the doctor confirmed it: she was pregnant.

Tears welled in Mira's eyes. Aarav gently held her hand. In that quiet clinic room, filled with soft fluorescent light and the muffled sounds of life outside, their world shifted.

They were going to become parents.

Their home, once filled with plants and books and the aroma of evening tea, now brimmed with new excitement. Baby clothes arrived. The walls were repainted. Names were whispered. But amidst all the planning, one quiet, powerful suggestion from Mira's grandmother stood out.

"Don't just prepare the house," she said. "Prepare your soul. The child listens, learns, and waits for you."

That was when Mira and Aarav discovered Garbh Sanskar—the ancient wisdom that teaches not only how a mother shapes her child's body but also how her thoughts, emotions, and environment shape the soul quietly blooming inside her.

They immersed themselves in it—not out of obligation, but out of awe. Each day became a sacred dance of music, stories, yoga, meditation, and deep reflection. Mira often sat by the window, the morning sun warming her skin, gently caressing her belly, and speaking softly.

"Can you hear me, little one?"

One evening, Mira paused during meditation, her hand resting on her bump. And then—like a whisper rising from within—she *felt* something. Not just a movement but a presence. A quiet voice inside her heart.

"I can hear you, Ma. But more than hearing... I need you to understand me."

Tears slipped down Mira's cheeks.

"I'm not just a heartbeat in your womb," the soul whispered. "I'm conscious. I feel what you feel. When your mind is clouded, I tremble. When your heart sings, I glow. I am waiting—not just to be born, but to be known."

From that day, everything changed.

Mira's voice softened. Her days slowed down. Her laughter deepened. She stopped rushing. Instead, she listened—to herself, to the stillness, to the life within.

She wrote letters, sometimes at midnight, lit by a warm lamp.

"My beloved child, I don't know what the world will ask of you, but I want you to know that you are not alone. Even before you take your first breath, you are held, cherished, and seen."

Aarav, too, found new layers within himself. He began speaking to the child during his evening flute sessions, telling stories of courage and kindness. He believed each note, each story, was a thread weaving into their baby's soul.

And their child responded.

When Aarav played the flute, the baby kicked— rhythmic, soft taps, as if dancing. When Mira chanted Sanskrit mantras, the baby stilled, listening. When she cried one evening from fear and doubt, the baby turned restless, reminding her— "I feel it too."

One night, Mira had a dream so vivid it lingered even after waking. She was in a luminous garden, bathed in golden light. A radiant child walked toward her, smiling.

"I chose you," the child said. "Before you even knew me, I was waiting for your love. I remember the lullabies, the warmth of your hands, the stories. I remember *you*."

She woke up gasping, her heart full.

From then on, Garbh Sanskar wasn't a practice—it was a conversation. A bridge between worlds.

Finally, on a monsoon-drenched morning, Mira gave birth to a beautiful baby boy—Ayaan. As the nurse placed him on Mira's chest, she instinctively sang the lullaby she had sung every night during pregnancy. The baby's cries softened immediately. He gazed up at her with a quiet knowing, eyes full of awareness. It was as if he remembered everything.

In the days that followed, Mira and Aarav noticed little things—miracles in disguise. Ayaan was a calm, observant baby. He responded to familiar mantras and music with smiles and stillness. Unlike other newborns who were often unsettled, Ayaan seemed to carry peaceful energy, as though he had been gently carved by love even before he entered the world.

As he grew, his uniqueness became more visible. He began speaking earlier than most children, expressing empathy in ways that surprised even his grandparents. He would place his tiny hand on Mira's face when she looked tired or sit silently, listening to Aarav's stories with a seriousness far beyond his years.

At the age of three, Ayaan could recite Sanskrit shlokas with astonishing clarity, and he showed an innate interest in music, rhythm, and storytelling. He wasn't just intelligent—he was intuitive. He understood emotions, asked questions about the world, about kindness, about why people hurt, and how one could help.

Mira and Aarav often sat together at night, quietly watching Ayaan sleep. They felt something deeper than pride—it was reverence. The soul they had once spoken to through silence and song had become a child of wisdom, sensitivity, and light.

They realized that Garbh Sanskar had not only shaped Ayaan but had transformed them as well. It had taught them mindfulness, patience, and how to live intentionally. Their home was not just filled with laughter—it was filled with meaning.

At school, Ayaan stood out—not by being the loudest or the fastest—but through his depth. Teachers praised his compassion, his focus, and his ability to connect ideas with emotions. When he performed on stage, narrating ancient tales or playing the flute alongside his father, audiences were moved not just by his talent but by the grace he carried.

Mira remembered the dream again—the child in the golden garden. "I chose you," he had said. Now, she truly believed it. They hadn't just brought a child into the world. They had welcomed a soul who came with a purpose—and they had honoured it.

Even now, years later, Mira continues to write letters. Aarav still plays the flute in the evenings. And Ayaan, now a growing boy with dreams in his eyes, still feels the music of those unseen conversations—the sacred rhythm that began in the womb and continues to echo in the quiet moments of their lives.

And sometimes, just before falling asleep, Ayaan whispers to his mother, "Thank you for loving me before I even arrived. I remember everything."

Employer–Employee: The Power of Mutual Understanding

Sujay Patel had always been a high performer. As a Regional Manager, his name was synonymous with success. Month after month, his region posted record-breaking numbers. He was respected by his peers and loved by his clients. However, in the last few months, something had shifted. The spark was dimming. Performance was declining, meetings were more tense, and a cloud of low morale hung over the team.

His team—once full of energy and ideas—had grown quiet. Absenteeism was on the rise. Key talents were resigning, and the passion that once fuelled late nights and early mornings was nowhere to be found. The targets hadn't changed, but the people had. Something was deeply wrong, and Sujay knew the answer wasn't in spreadsheets or quarterly reviews.

It was emotional.

One Monday morning, Sujay stood in the conference room as his team filtered in for the weekly review. PowerPoint slides detailed targets, charts reflected dips, and discussions circled around tactics. But behind the numbers, Sujay sensed something deeper—exhaustion, frustration, and resignation.

So, he did something unexpected.

He turned off the projector.

"No charts today," he said quietly. "I want to talk about us—how we're feeling, what's working, and what isn't. No judgments. Just honesty."

There was silence. Then, slowly, it started. A junior executive spoke about the mental exhaustion from back-to-back calls. Another mentioned how favouritism was creating resentment. Someone else shared their fear of being fired despite working 14-hour days. And finally, a senior rep admitted, "I love this job, but I don't love how it makes me feel anymore."

Sujay felt the room shift. This was no longer about performance metrics. It was about people.

Over the next few weeks, Sujay dove into the emotional landscape of his team. He held one-on-one conversations, launched anonymous surveys, and even hosted informal team lunches where work talk was banned. The results painted a sobering picture:

Excessive meetings were leaving no time for ground-level work or client interaction.

Favouritism was quietly eroding team morale, with top performers overlooked in Favour of 'favourites.

Workload pressures were sky-high due to a lack of hiring, pushing employees toward burnout.

Incentives and recognition were unclear or absent, leading to disengagement.

Job insecurity fostered fear, not growth.

Toxic leadership behaviours went unaddressed, and feedback rarely travelled upwards.

The lack of emotional connection between management and the team had left people feeling like cogs in a machine.

Sujay knew now: these weren't just HR issues— they were psychological issues.

Human behaviour is driven not only by incentives but also by emotions. When people feel safe, seen, and valued, their performance elevates; when they feel ignored, threatened, or unrecognized, motivation crumbles.

Sujay started reading extensively—books on organizational psychology, emotional intelligence, and the neuroscience of motivation. One quote stood out to him:

"People don't quit jobs; they quit emotional environments."

He realized the organization had been focusing too much on output and too little on emotional input.

Armed with insights, Sujay developed a people-first turnaround strategy. Not a single performance target was changed—only the way people were treated.

✓ Meetings were cut down by 60%. Only essential calls were held. More time was given for field work and real customer interaction. Managers, too, were encouraged to spend time on the ground to understand realities firsthand.

✓ A transparent performance-tracking system was implemented. Growth opportunities, key accounts, and recognitions were based solely on merit. The message was clear: results mattered, not relationships.

✓ Sujay pushed for strategic hiring. Realistic targets were reset after team discussions. He involved team leaders in workload planning to ensure fairness.

✓ A dual-layer recognition system was introduced:

• Public Appreciation: Weekly shout-outs, monthly awards, and internal newsletters celebrated top performers.

• Private Gratitude: Sujay personally thanked employees, sometimes with handwritten notes—a rare act that deeply touched many.

✓ No work-related calls after 6 PM. Weekends were declared sacred. A weekly "Recharge Friday" was introduced, where employees could sign off early to invest time in personal wellbeing.

✓ Toxic managers were given an ultimatum: change or exit. Leadership development workshops were conducted with a focus on empathy, communication, and emotional intelligence. Sujay made sure that leadership wasn't about control but about connection.

✓ Techniques and workflows were refined through market analysis, competitor benchmarking, and creative campaigns. The focus shifted from quantity to quality of effort.

✓ Regular training sessions improved product knowledge and team skills. More importantly, sessions included mental wellness, time management, and handling failure.

✓ An open-door policy allowed anyone to approach Sujay without hierarchy. Monthly anonymous feedback was read aloud, and action was taken transparently.

Sujay took a step further. He understood that employees were not just professionals—they were parents, caregivers, students, and human beings with complex lives.

He introduced:

Emergency Leave Without Questions: No justification needed—just trust.

Personal Milestone Celebrations: Birthdays, anniversaries, and even children's achievements were acknowledged.

Mental Health Check-ins: Access to counsellors and emotional support resources.

His managers were trained in empathic listening so they could hear what wasn't being said.

One manager later shared: "I realized that when an employee's performance dips, I shouldn't ask 'Why didn't you do it?' but rather, 'Are you okay?'"

Trust became the foundation of every interaction. When employees were trusted with flexibility, they responded with loyalty. When they were allowed to prioritize personal commitments without guilt, they returned to work more focused, creative, and committed. By letting people be human, the organization was building professionals who cared—not just about targets but about the team and the vision.

Sujay encouraged everyone to maintain a healthy boundary between work and life. He reminded his team, "We work to live, not live to work." Employees were given space to attend family events, rest when needed, or take mental health breaks. This simple shift created a ripple effect—relationships improved, burnout reduced, and joy returned to the workplace.

But the transformation wasn't just for the employees.

Even those in higher management began to change. Sujay, too, felt lighter. The burden of control gave way to the peace of connection. Leaders started experiencing less anxiety and more clarity. Managers who once micromanaged began collaborating. They started listening, not just managing. Understanding their teams gave them deeper satisfaction and a sense of purpose beyond profits.

One senior leader admitted in a review meeting, "Earlier, I thought leadership was about making people work harder. Now I know—it's about helping people feel safe, and the results follow naturally."

As trust blossomed, so did emotional safety. People were no longer afraid to speak up or ask for help. The culture matured from performance pressure to performance partnership. Sujay had proved that trust wasn't earned through policies—it was nurtured through genuine human connection.

Six months later, the numbers told a new story:

📈 Results rose by 40%—not due to increased pressure, but reduced toxicity.

📈 Attrition dropped by 60%. People stayed not because they had to but because they wanted to.

📈 Employee engagement scores hit record highs.

📈 Client satisfaction improved—happy employees treated clients better.

But more than metrics, the culture had transformed. Laughter returned to the workplace. Brainstorming replaced blame. Compassion coexisted with competition.

One evening, after a long but satisfying day, Sujay sat reflecting in his office. A quote from a recent training session echoed in his mind:

"No one can fully understand you in every situation. But those who try to make all the difference."

He had learned that leadership wasn't about being right. It was about being real. About seeing people not just as employees but as humans. About realizing that numbers follow emotions—not the other way around.

Sujay's journey became a case study in the organization. But to him, it wasn't a strategy—it was humanity.

Now, everyone is happy and has started feeling, *"Somebody finally understands me."*

🔑 Final Lesson:

Build a culture where people feel seen, heard, and valued. Because when employers and employees genuinely understand each other, success becomes effortless—and human.

Understanding the Unseen: One Woman's Truth Beyond Poverty

Mira's day began long before the sun kissed the sky. In the quiet hush of dawn, she slowly stirred from her sleep, careful not to wake her children—Ayaan and Riya—who were curled up beside her on their shared mattress. Their house was modest: two small rooms with faded walls and a tin roof that clattered in the rain. But inside, it breathed warmth, care, and the faint fragrance of hope.

As she tiptoed into the small kitchen, she wrapped her shawl tighter around her shoulders. The floor was cold, but her heart was steady. She boiled water for tea and kneaded dough for flatbreads while her mind ran in parallel—mentally dividing her income, counting her savings in whispers: *"Ten rupees saved yesterday... maybe fifty this week. Someday, I'll fix that leaking roof. Someday, I'll buy Riya her own study table. Someday, I'll build a real home—not just walls, but dreams tucked into every corner."*

Mira packed simple lunches—rice, dal, a few cooked vegetables—and slipped handwritten notes in Ayaan and Riya's tiffin like she always did. Just a little heart or a message: *"Be kind. Study hard. I'm proud of you."*

By six o'clock, she woke them up with gentle strokes on their hair and a whisper that carried more love than any lullaby. "Wake up, my stars. Let's not keep your future waiting. After dropping them off at school, Mira began her long day. She worked in four different houses—cleaning, scrubbing, cooking. Her hands bore the story of her life—cracked palms, callused fingers—but her face never lost its light. She smiled easily, even when her back ached, even when her legs trembled by evening. Her dreams weren't extravagant. She didn't yearn for gold or silk. She dreamt of giving her children an education, a life where they wouldn't have to wake before dawn or count coins to buy notebooks. She dreamed of evenings spent in a small home with laughter and no worries. A home where Ayaan could become an engineer and Riya a teacher.

"I want them to be respected," she often thought, *"not pitied. I don't want them to carry the weight of my struggles—I carry it so they can be free."*

Every month, she tucked away a few notes in a box under her bed—a secret treasure. Sometimes five rupees, sometimes ten. That box held more than money. It held her patience. Her vision. Her silent prayers.

One of the houses she worked in belonged to the Roy family—wealthy, well-respected. Mira had served them for five years with quiet devotion. Mrs. Roy often said, "Mira, I don't trust many, but I trust you."

But despite that trust, they never really *saw* Mira. They saw her work, her hands, her discipline— but not her heart. Not the mother who went hungry so her kids could eat a little more. Not the woman who skipped medicines so she could pay for a school notebook. Not the one who stitched her torn slippers with thread, whispering to herself, *"Next month... maybe next month, I'll buy new ones."*

Then, one day, everything changed.

A diamond necklace went missing. A storm of chaos swept through the Roy household. The servants were questioned, cupboards searched, and drawers overturned.

And then the whisper began.

"She's the only outsider."

"She's poor, desperate... maybe Mira took it."

When Mrs. Roy called Mira into the hall, her voice was strained.

"Mira... we've trusted you, but the necklace is missing. Did you... did you take it?"

The words struck like cold steel. Mira's breath caught. Her eyes welled up—not from guilt, but from pain.

"Madam," she said softly, her voice trembling, "I barely earn enough to buy a new pair of shoes for my children. But I've never taken what isn't mine. Not even a coin."

Still, the seed of doubt had taken root. Mr. Roy called the police.

Mira stood frozen as officers searched her bag. Her children had come running, sensing something wrong. Riya clung to her hand, trembling. "My mom is not a thief!" she shouted, eyes fierce.

And then... silence broke.

A small voice spoke up. Ravi, the helper boy who worked quietly in the house, looked nervous but stepped forward. "Madam... I saw something. The cat... it was playing near the dressing table. It had something shiny in its mouth."

Everyone turned.

A frantic search led to the base of a heavy wardrobe. There, dusty and hidden, lay the missing necklace.

Mrs. Roy stood stunned. Guilt washed over her face. "Mira... I'm so sorry. I should have believed you."

Mira stood tall. Not angry. Just tired. "Madam, all I own is my integrity. That's what feeds my soul when money runs short. Today, it protected me."

She turned to Mr. Roy. "Sir, poverty isn't a crime. Being poor doesn't make us thieves. Our struggles don't make us dishonest. What we lack in money, we make up for in dignity."

And in that moment, something shifted in the Roys. For the first time, they truly saw Mira, not as help, not as the woman who worked quietly in the background, but as a person—a mother, a dreamer, a fighter. They had never tried to understand her emotions, her silence, her strength. They had trusted her work but not her soul.

Mrs. Roy wiped her tears. "You're right, Mira. What happened to you was wrong. We doubted your character, not understanding your life and your values. Please forgive us."

That day changed more than perceptions. Mr. and Mrs. Roy offered Mira free vocational training—so she could learn and grow and build a better future, not as charity but as recognition of her resilience and worth.

Weeks passed. The incident faded from people's memories—but not from hearts. And then, one afternoon, while Mira was folding clothes in the Roys' living room, she heard a soft thud from upstairs. Rushing up, she found Mrs. Roy unconscious near the staircase.

There was no one else at home—Mr. Roy was out of town, their children were abroad, and the house staff had left for errands.

Mira's hands trembled for a moment, but her mind became sharp. She quickly called an auto-rickshaw, lifted Mrs. Roy into it with help from the driver, and rushed her to the nearest hospital. "Chest pain... she fainted," she told the doctor, barely catching her breath. She gave every detail the hospital needed, stayed through the admission, and signed the papers with her trembling hands—taking responsibility without hesitation.

Doctors confirmed it was a mild heart attack. Because Mira had brought her in quickly, her life had been saved.

For the next several days, Mira stayed by her side in the hospital. She fed her, comforted her, and massaged her hands when they ached from IV drips. She read her the newspaper, told her stories, and even made her laugh. Mira didn't leave—even though her own home, her kids, and her work all demanded her presence.

Mrs. Roy, recovering slowly, held her hand one evening and whispered with tears, "You could've walked away. We doubted you. We hurt you. But you saved my life."

Mira simply smiled. "Madam, you made a mistake. But I didn't forget who I am. I know what pain feels like. I'll never let someone suffer alone if I can help it. Especially someone I've shared life with for so many years."

That night, Mrs. Roy cried—not from illness, but from gratitude. For the first time, she saw the full depth of Mira's heart.

Mira returned home after Mrs. Roy recovered. Her children welcomed her with warm food and warm hugs.

The Roy family never again saw Mira as 'help.' They saw her as a human being full of grace and quiet strength—a woman whose heart had lifted more weight than most could imagine.

Truth and honesty are silent warriors. They may not shine immediately, but in time, they win. If you stay true to your values, the world will learn to see you—not for your poverty, but for your strength. Even the smallest dreams can stand tall when built on the foundation of integrity. And sometimes, in this unfair world, goodness finds its way back to those who give it—even when it's undeserved.

Friends in the Crossfire: *A story of unspoken truths, quiet resilience, and love beyond labels*

Sameera and Vikram met in their final year of college—not through a dramatic twist of fate, but over spilled coffee and a shared hatred for early morning lectures. She was sharp, introspective, and always scribbling quotes in the margins of her books.

He was full of heart and spontaneity, dreaming big without apology. What started as casual banter turned into long walks, late-night debates, and a connection built not on similarity but on curiosity.

They were never a couple, but something deeper simmered beneath the surface. Not romance—just raw, unfiltered presence. They knew each other's rhythms, moods, and silences like second skin.

Life, as it does, pulled them in different directions after college. Vikram dove headfirst into advertising. His charisma and creativity earned him quick promotions. He thrived in chaos, working late, leading campaigns, and charming clients.

Sameera, on the other hand, struggled. After a brief stint at a magazine, she took a break to care for her mental health. The break turned into years. Her days were quieter, filled with freelance gigs, therapy sessions, journaling, and long spells of self-doubt.

They kept in touch—texts, voice notes, and occasional coffee meetups. But over time, the gap between their worlds widened.

Vikram didn't see how hard Sameera was fighting just to get out of bed some mornings. Sameera didn't tell him. She didn't want to be a burden.

And Vikram never talked about the panic attacks that started after he got promoted. He didn't think he was allowed to feel lost when everyone saw him as a rising star.

Things reached a boiling point when Vikram got a national award for a campaign he led. His social media was flooded with congratulations. Sameera liked the post. She even commented: "Proud of you!" But something inside her felt like crumbling.

They met a few days later for dinner.

The conversation was stilted. Sameera tried to mask her feelings with sarcasm. Vikram was distracted and tired and failed to see through it.

"Must be nice," she muttered at one point, "to be so celebrated."

"What's that supposed to mean?" he asked.

"Nothing," she said. But everything was packed in that word.

Later that night, Vikram called her out. "Why do I feel like you're angry with me all the time?"

"I'm not," she said. But her voice betrayed her.

They didn't speak for weeks after that.

The silence stretched. Both waited for the other to make a move. Sameera withdrew further, convinced she was being left behind. Vikram felt betrayed—was his success something to be ashamed of now?

During this time, they both began journaling—ironically, the same coping method they once laughed about. Each entry was filled with questions, and neither of them had the courage to ask aloud.

Then came the text that changed everything.

"Do we even know each other anymore?" Sameera had written. No reply for hours. Then finally: "I don't know. But I want to. Can we talk?"

They met not at a café but at the old college library steps—the place where it all began.

Sameera spoke first. Her voice trembled.

"I've been angry. At myself. At the world. And I didn't know how to be around your success without feeling like I was drowning."

Vikram looked down. "I've been scared too. I didn't know how to talk about my struggles without sounding ungrateful. And I hated that I was scared of your silence."

Their conversation stretched into the night. They laughed. They cried. They apologized. They admitted what neither had dared to say for years: that they missed each other—not just physically, but emotionally.

Healing didn't happen overnight. But they chose to rebuild—with intention.

They began new rituals. Monthly check-ins. Letter-writing (actual handwritten ones). Weekly voice notes. And a pact: speak from honesty, not ego.

Sometimes, healing looked like this: Sameera reading her poetry aloud to Vikram over the phone. Vikram listened quietly, whispering, "That's beautiful" after every verse. Or Vikram calling her after a long meeting just to hear her say something real. Something grounding.

There was no possessiveness. No conditions. Their friendship was a sanctuary, untouchable by jealousy, untouched by greed.

It was the kind of bond where you didn't need to say, "I love you." You showed it by showing up. Again and again.

One winter evening, after lighting lamps for Diwali at their respective homes, Sameera called Vikram.

"I lit one extra diya for you," she said softly. "For peace. For light to find you when I can't."

Vikram's voice caught. "I lit one for you, too. For stillness. You carry so much."

They didn't call it divine. But what they had was sacred.

When Sameera lost her father, Vikram came to the funeral not to speak but to sit by her in silence. Later, as the rituals ended, he folded her father's favourite shawl and placed it in her hands. "So he can still be around your shoulders when it's cold," he said.

She cried—not from grief, but from being seen.

Years passed. And their lives took shapes neither had imagined.

Sameera published her second book—a collection of essays on healing, solitude, and soul friendships. The dedication read:

"To Vikram—my forever mirror. You never tried to fix me. You only held space for me to unfold."

When Vikram launched his mental wellness initiative, Sameera wrote the mission statement: "To remind the world that strength looks like softness, and success is meaningless without someone to share your truth with."

At an interview, someone asked them, "You both never married. Did you ever fall in love with each other?"

Sameera smiled, then looked at Vikram. "Of course we did. Just not the kind you write love songs about. The kind you whisper prayers for."

Vikram nodded, eyes moist. "We didn't need to belong to each other. We just chose to walk with each other."

They never grew old alone. They grew old together—in different homes, different cities, but forever entwined in a kind of quiet, holy devotion.

No romance. Just reverence.

Not untouched by fire—but forged in it and purified by grace.

Their friendship became a soul's resting place. A space where neither had to explain their pain nor shrink their joy.

People often asked them how they stayed so close through the years—through changes, challenges, and silences.

They would always smile, sometimes even chuckle gently, and say the same thing: "We listened harder when it got uncomfortable. That's how we stayed."

Because in the end, the love between Sameera and Vikram didn't need labels, declarations, or timelines.

It simply was—steady, patient, and deeply human.

And if anyone asked what the secret truly was, the answer would always come softly but firmly:

It was the result of understanding each other—deeply.

Generational Gaps

Grandfather and Anaya: A Clash of Values

Grandfather, with his silver hair and wise eyes, often found solace in the simplicity of his traditional values. He cherished the rituals and customs that had been passed down through generations, believing they were the essence of family and culture. Anaya, his spirited granddaughter, represented a different world, one filled with modern ideas and technology. Their relationship was a tapestry woven with love yet fraught with tension as they navigated the chasm between Grandfather's traditionalism and Anaya's contemporary outlook. Conflicts arose subtly but surely, ignited by Anaya's choices in lifestyle, clothing, and friendships, which often clashed with Grandfather's expectations.

One afternoon, the conflict reached its peak during a family gathering. Anaya arrived wearing jeans and a vibrant crop top, while Grandfather had hoped she would don the traditional salwar kameez he had gifted her for such occasions. As the family sat down for lunch, Grandfather's disapproving gaze lingered on Anaya, who was engrossed in her phone, sharing moments from the event on social media. "Can somebody understand me?" he wondered silently, feeling the weight of a time when family gatherings were about connection, not digital distractions. The tension was palpable; Anaya sensed her grandfather's disappointment but couldn't comprehend why her choice of attire and her connection to friends via social media was seen as disrespectful.

The misunderstanding deepened when Grandfather confronted Anaya about her lifestyle, emphasizing the importance of tradition and respect for elders. Anaya, frustrated by his rigidity, retorted those times had changed. "Grandpa, I love you, but I want to express myself in ways that resonate with my generation," she exclaimed, her voice rising. Grandfather, feeling rejected and misunderstood, retreated into silence, believing that Anaya was losing touch with her roots. This moment crystallized the generational divide, highlighting how differing values could create chasms in relationships that seemed insurmountable.

However, the turning point came when Anaya decided to engage her grandfather in an open conversation. She invited him to join her for a walk in the park, a place where they could talk without the distractions of family expectations. As they strolled among the blooming flowers, Anaya shared her perspective, explaining how social media helped her connect with friends and express her individuality. She asked Grandfather about his childhood, encouraging him to share stories of his youth, which were rich with tradition but also filled with his dreams and aspirations. "Can somebody understand me?" she asked again, this time reaching out for his understanding rather than his approval.

Grandfather listened, his heart softening as he realized that while Anaya's choices were different, they were not disrespectful. He began to share his own experiences of rebellion against traditions in his youth, drawing parallels between their lives. This exchange of stories fostered empathy and understanding, bridging the gap between their values. Grandfather came to appreciate Anaya's desire for self-expression, and Anaya recognized the significance of the traditions that Grandfather held dear. They found common ground in their love for each other, allowing them to navigate their differences with respect and compassion.

Through heartfelt conversations and shared experiences, Grandfather and Anaya learned to embrace their differences as strengths rather than sources of conflict. They established a new understanding: traditions could coexist with modernity. Grandfather began to appreciate Anaya's vibrant spirit, while Anaya grew to respect the wisdom in her grandfather's beliefs.

Their relationship blossomed into a beautiful blend of old and new, showcasing that despite the clash of values, love and understanding could pave the way for resolution and harmony in their hearts.

Bridging Tradition and Modernity

The intersection of tradition and modernity often becomes a breeding ground for conflict in relationships, particularly within families. This dynamic is vividly illustrated in the story of Grandfather and his granddaughter, Anaya. Grandfather, deeply rooted in his traditional values, struggles to understand Anaya's modern lifestyle, which includes social media and a less formal approach to relationships. Their conflicts often arise when Grandfather criticizes Anaya's choices, questioning her commitment to family traditions. Anaya, feeling misunderstood, frequently wonders, "Can somebody understand me?" This poignant question encapsulates her frustration as she navigates her desire for independence while respecting her grandfather's values.

As the tension escalates, a pivotal moment occurs when Anaya decides to invite Grandfather to her college's cultural festival. Initially reluctant, he ultimately agrees, motivated by a desire to connect with her world. The festival serves as a bridge between their contrasting lifestyles. Through shared experiences, they engage in conversations that reveal their vulnerabilities. Anaya explains her perspective on modern friendships and career aspirations, while Grandfather shares stories from his youth, shedding light on the values he holds dear. This exchange fosters empathy as both characters begin to see the merits of each other's worlds. The resolution lies not in choosing one lifestyle over another but in finding common ground that honors both tradition and modernity.

The Workplace Dilemma: Rohan and Priya – Navigating Power Dynamics

Rohan and Priya's story began in the bustling workspace of a tech firm that thrived on precision and deadlines. Rohan, the seasoned project manager, was known for his calm efficiency and ability to drive performance. Priya, a quiet and deeply thoughtful software developer, had only recently joined the team but quickly gained attention for her technical skills and dedication. Rohan noticed her potential early and began assigning her to critical, high-stakes projects—ones he knew required both technical brilliance and quiet resilience.

At first, Priya was honoured by the trust. Every new assignment felt like an opportunity to prove herself, to grow in the eyes of her manager and perhaps even in her own. She believed that good work would be seen, appreciated, and rewarded. The long nights, the skipped lunches, the silent sacrifice—she told herself it was part of the process. She took the pressure without complaint, wearing her performance like a silent badge of honour.

Slowly, a pattern began to emerge—one she had tried to ignore at first. While she was carrying the weight of complex system migrations and customer-facing backend fixes, some of her equally capable peers were working on routine feature updates or cosmetic enhancements. They had time to take breaks and talk about their weekends. Priya, on the other hand, often found herself the last one to log off, her eyes dry and her mind heavy.

What made it harder were the whispers—the comments from colleagues that weren't necessarily cruel but certainly weren't kind. "Oh, another top-priority task for Priya," one of them said in a tone laced with sarcasm. Another joked, "We should all change our names to Priya. Maybe then we'll get real work." She laughed along. But it hurt. It hurt deeply. The very thing she thought would make her feel proud—being trusted and relied upon—was now isolating her from the team.

Still, she didn't speak up. She thought maybe it was just a phase. Maybe she had to try harder. Be stronger.

Outside the office, Priya's life was quiet and solitary. She had moved to the city recently, leaving behind her family and close friends. Her small apartment was a mix of silence and soft music, her only escape from the pressure cooker at work. She often spoke to her mother on weekends, brushing off questions about stress with a practiced smile. Her calendar was filled with deadlines, not dinner plans. The loneliness crept in, uninvited, and stayed.

Rohan, on the other hand, had a family—a supportive wife, two young kids, and a home filled with the chaos of joy. But even his evenings were often interrupted by emails and Slack notifications. He was deeply committed to his work, believing that his drive was for the betterment of the team. What he didn't realize was that his belief in silent resilience—that work spoke for itself—was quietly hurting someone he truly respected.

Back in the team, murmurs of dissatisfaction were growing. Some members felt neglected; others misunderstood. A few admired Priya but also resented the seeming favouritism. One team member, Neha, who had been on the team for over a year, began to feel invisible. "Why does Priya get all the good projects?"

she asked in a feedback session. "Does the rest of the team even matter?" These concerns rarely reached Rohan directly. They lived in hallway conversations and WhatsApp group chats.

Then came the project that broke the rhythm. A multi-phase rollout, with shifting requirements and urgent cross-functional dependencies, landed squarely in Priya's lap while she was still untangling a previous deployment. She tried to speak up. Tried to say that her plate was full. But Rohan, with a friendly smile, said, "If anyone can pull this off, it's you." He meant it as praise. She heard it as pressure. Once again, she nodded, not because she was ready, but because she didn't feel like she had a choice.

She worked nights. Skipped meals. Watched her calendar fill with urgent meetings and last-minute calls. She knew she was close to burning out, but she kept going. Until one morning, it happened. The demo she was supposed to deliver—one she had rehearsed endlessly—had to be postponed. The backend integration had failed during QA. It wasn't entirely her fault, but in the final review meeting, Rohan's voice cut sharp through the Zoom call.

"I expected better from you, Priya."

Just six words. But it felt like a verdict.

She didn't cry. Didn't react. She just turned off her camera, muted herself, and stared at the screen. Numb. That evening, she sat alone in her apartment, not touching her food. Her mind played the scene on repeat. For all the work she had done, all the weekends she had lost—this is what it had come to.

After that day, something in her shifted. She stopped offering suggestions in meetings. Stopped going the extra mile. She still did her work, but there was no spark, no ownership. She began browsing job sites during lunch breaks. Maybe it was time to leave— not just the team, but the company. She felt invisible, used, and, worst of all, misunderstood.

Meanwhile, Rohan began to notice the change. Priya's enthusiasm had vanished. Team morale overall felt sluggish. Tasks were being completed, but the energy was off. He began to wonder—had he pushed her too far? Had he missed something?

He replayed the demo meeting in his mind, remembering how casually he had thrown those words. At the time, it felt like a simple statement of disappointment. Now, he saw it through a different lens. Had he unintentionally dismissed everything she had been holding up?

He scheduled a one-on-one with her. She considered cancelling it. What was left to say? What could change now?

But curiosity—and maybe a flicker of hope—held her back.

They met in a quiet corner room. No interruptions. No screens. Just two people and a silence that felt heavy with everything left unsaid.

Rohan began, not with reprimand or feedback, but with something different.

"I feel like I may have made things harder for you without realizing it," he said softly. "I'd really like to understand where I went wrong."

Her guard didn't drop immediately. But those words cracked open something inside her. She began to speak—not angrily, not tearfully—but truthfully.

She told him about the weight she carried. The projects. The pressure. The subtle alienation. The loneliness of being seen only when things went wrong. She told him how his silence, his failure to check in, made her feel like a machine and not a person. She even told him about the day he publicly said he expected better. "It wasn't just criticism," she explained. "It felt like you didn't see me at all."

Rohan didn't defend himself. He listened. And he apologized—not for the missed deadline, but for missing *her*.

That conversation changed them both.

Rohan went back to his leadership playbook and tore out the old pages. He began holding regular check-ins—not just to track performance but to understand how his team was feeling. He introduced a rotation policy for high-impact projects to balance the load. In team meetings, he started recognizing not just outcomes but effort. And for the first time in months, the team began smiling again.

Priya stayed.

Not because everything became perfect overnight but because someone had finally listened. Seen her. Understood her.

She started mentoring new hires. Speaking up in retrospectives. She even co-led a company-wide workshop with Rohan called "Understanding the

Human Side of Work," where they told their story—not as hero and victim—but as two people who got lost in the noise of performance and pressure and found their way back through honesty.

They began encouraging team members to be open about burnout signs, to ask for help without fear, and to see feedback not just as correction—but as connection. Trust began to flow back into the team, little by little.

The team, too, began to shift. Neha was invited to lead a strategic module. Others were looped into decision-making processes. A quiet revolution began—driven not by KPIs or OKRs—but by empathy.

Looking back now, Priya realizes that the hardest part wasn't the workload. It was the silence. The assumptions. The invisible emotional labour of always being the strong one.

And Rohan? He learned that good leadership isn't about assigning tasks—it's about acknowledging the humans who carry them.

In the end, the distance between misunderstanding and connection wasn't as wide as it once seemed. It was one honest conversation away.

And for both of them, it made all the difference.

The Art of Being Siblings

A Story of Rivalry, Realization, and Reconnection

Sibling rivalry often unfolds in complicated, silent ways. For Neha and Karan, it began quietly—little comparisons at dinner, a few more claps for one report card over the other, and a subtle tilt in tone when achievements were mentioned.

"You got an A again, Neha?" their mother would beam. "So proud of you!"

Karan would stir his rice, eyes downcast. "I improved in history," he'd say softly.

"That's nice," their father would reply, already turning back to Neha. "But Neha, that science score! Incredible."

It wasn't that anyone meant harm. But slowly, the warmth between the siblings began to thin. Neha climbed the academic ladder effortlessly. Karan found his rhythm elsewhere—art, music, random DIY projects—but those things rarely made it to the dinner table.

Yet, in truth, their parents had tried—really tried—to raise them with love that felt equal. From the time they were toddlers, their father made it a point to give them "together time"—bedtime stories read with one child on each arm, puzzle games that only worked when played in pairs, and weekly "sibling missions," where they were asked to build something or complete a scavenger hunt together.

Their mother had her own rituals—morning lunches packed with little notes: *"Help each other today." "Neha, listen to your brother's story." "Karan, cheer your sister on."* She believed that children who felt heard at home wouldn't need to compete for love.

And it worked for a while. Neha and Karan had a language of inside jokes, team chants for every school event, and matching sketchbooks they filled together. Their parents watched proudly as the two formed not just a bond but what seemed like a fortress of friendship.

The family played board games on weekends around the living room table. Neha was competitive, and Karan was more easygoing. When Neha got frustrated with a loss, Karan would nudge her playfully and say, "Hey, I'll win next time *for* you." Their parents would glance at each other, hopeful.

But time is sneaky. Academic pressure crept in. Recognition started to tilt more toward measurable achievement—marks, medals, rankings. Without realizing it, their well-meaning encouragement turned lopsided.

"Neha topped her class again!" they'd announce proudly at family gatherings, while Karan's art competition win would be a quiet mention over dessert.

And slowly, despite the foundation of love, cracks began to show.

Before the rivalry took root, Neha and Karan were inseparable in their little rituals. On Sunday mornings, they would sit on the porch steps with mugs of hot chocolate—Neha's with cinnamon, Karan's plain—and talk about everything from comic books to the weird dreams they had the night before. They'd cycle to the corner shop together, share fries, and tease each other over silly things like who ran faster or who could whistle louder.

Karan once painted a wall in Neha's room with a galaxy mural for her birthday, spending three nights working in secret. She called it her "dream wall" and swore she'd never repaint it. That same night, she stayed up helping him rewrite a poem he was nervous about submitting for a school competition. "You're a better writer than you think," she had whispered. That was them—supportive, playful, quietly protective.

But as they entered high school, the rhythm shifted. Neha's achievements piled up—trophies, certificates, applause at every award function. Karan, still creative and capable, began to feel like the background character in his own home.

Everything came to a head during their final year of school when both of them applied for the same scholarship.

"You're applying too?" Neha asked one evening, trying to sound casual.

Karan nodded, almost defiantly. "Yeah. Why not?"

She hesitated, unsure if it was pride or fear in his voice. "Nothing... I just thought—"

"That I wouldn't?" he snapped. "That it's out of my league?"

"I didn't say that," she muttered, guilt blooming in her chest.

Weeks passed in tense silence. The teasing stopped. The bike rides ended. Meals became quiet. Then the day arrived.

Neha burst into the living room, waving the email on her phone. "I got it! The scholarship!"

Their parents rushed over, hugging her, proud smiles stretching ear to ear. Karan stood at the edge of the room, stiff.

"I worked hard, too, you know," he mumbled.

Neha turned, surprised. "Karan—what are you talking about?"

He met her eyes, something brittle in his voice. "Never mind. You wouldn't get it."

She opened her mouth to speak, but he walked past her, brushing against her shoulder, his voice low and trembling.

"Can somebody understand me?"

That night, their mother stood at the sink, hands unmoving under running water. "Did we do this?" she asked quietly.

Their father leaned against the counter. "We did our best. But maybe... we didn't listen closely enough."

Family dinners turned quiet. Karan stopped showing up at breakfast. Neha would peek into his room and find the door shut and headphones in place. Even the hot chocolate mugs on Sundays disappeared.

One evening, as their parents talked about Neha's college plans, Karan set his spoon down a little too hard.

"You know I exist too, right?"

Their father blinked. "Of course you do. But this is Neha's big moment."

"It's always her moment," he said, standing up. "Every single time."

He left the table in silence. Neha watched him go, her appetite gone.

The ache of their fractured bond followed Neha even into her private world—her sketchbooks. Late one night, she sat hunched over a charcoal piece, the face of a girl caught between two shadows. One wore a medal. The other held a paintbrush.

"Still awake?" her father's voice startled her.

She quickly shut the book. "Just... working on something."

He sat beside her. "You really should get some rest. Big engineering orientation coming up."

"Dad," she said suddenly. "What if I don't want to go?"

He frowned. "What do you mean?"

She took a breath. "What if I want to be an artist?"

A silence. Not angry—just long, like a held breath.

"Neha, art is... beautiful, sure. But it's not a career. You're smart. You've worked hard for this. Why would you throw it away?"

Her voice cracked. "Because it's not me. It's what you want, not what I want."

"Neha..." he began, unsure.

"I just—" she wiped her eyes— "I wish someone would understand me."

He stared at her then. Really stared. And in her words, he heard an echo—Karan's echo.

That night, he turned to his wife and said, "We forgot something. We taught them to chase success, but we never reminded them that they were enough just as they are."

The next weekend, their parents called a family meeting—unusual, awkward, but necessary.

"We made mistakes," their mother began gently. "In trying to encourage you both, we forgot to really see you."

Their father nodded. "Karan, I'm sorry for all the times we made you feel second. And Neha... I never asked what you wanted. I only assumed."

Karan looked down, fingers clasped tight. "It's not just about the scholarship. It's everything. All I ever heard was how great Neha was."

"I didn't mean to make you feel like that," Neha said quietly. "I was so caught up in making them proud... I forgot to check on you."

"I wanted to matter too," he whispered.

"You *do* matter," she said, voice trembling. "I see it now. And I'll keep reminding you until you believe it."

Their father turned to Neha. "You said you want to be an artist."

She nodded slowly.

He exhaled. "Then we'll figure it out. It's scary for me—but maybe that's okay. Your happiness matters more than my fear."

The house changed after that. Not overnight. But in the quiet ways that matter.

Karan started showing Neha his music mixes. She complimented his style without a hint of condescension. Neha hung one of her sketches on the living room wall—her father framed it himself.

They brought back hot chocolate on Sundays. This time, they added a third mug—for their mother, who always claimed she was "too busy" before. Now, she sat between them, smiling.

The old rivalry dissolved into something new: respect.

And whenever the doubts crept in—when Neha questioned her future or Karan questioned his worth—they had each other.

They had a home where the question *"Can somebody understand me?"* no longer felt like a cry into the void.

It was a question that finally had an answer.

Across Borders, Between Hearts

I used to believe love could conquer anything. Then, I fell for someone who made me question where love ends and culture begins.

Rahul was everything I didn't know I needed—curious, passionate, unapologetically himself. He was North India wrapped in laughter and rebellion. I was South India—rituals and reverence tucked into every thread of my saree.

When he met my family, I thought I saw magic. But I also saw cracks.

He wore the Vashti like a costume. Spoke of pujas like parodies. Made my grandmother's beliefs sound outdated. That night, I looked in the mirror and whispered, *"Can someone understand me?"*

But I didn't ask him to. I expected him to just know.

And he didn't.

The more we clashed over wedding rituals and family expectations, the more isolated I felt inside the very relationship I used to celebrate. We loved each other deeply. But we forgot that love needs translation too—across cultures, across childhoods, across unspoken fears.

One day, during a heated conversation about guest lists and ceremonies, he said, "Why does everything have to be about *your* way, Aisha?"

I snapped. "Because my way is the only one I've ever known. Because it matters. Because it's who I am!"

He went quiet. And I cried for the first time—not because he didn't understand, but because I hadn't tried to make him understand without expecting him to already know.

It wasn't until I visited his home and saw the glint of pride in his eyes as his mother sang folk songs and his uncle roasted peanuts at Lohri that I understood what I had failed to see. *His culture wasn't lighter than mine. It was just different.*

So we rebuilt—from scratch.

We stopped trying to win. We started listening. We cried through misunderstandings and danced through our differences. Our wedding was a blend: jasmine and marigolds, dosas and chaats, Sanskrit chants and Punjabi beats.

It wasn't perfect. But it was us.

They say love is patient. But no one tells you that patience can feel like waiting in the dark, wondering if you've already been left behind.

Aarav was my long-distance lighthouse—steady, warm, and always just far enough to need squinting.

We met during a project in Mumbai. The connection was electric. But he went back to his city, and I flew back to mine—Singapore, where skyscrapers touched clouds, but my nights touched loneliness.

For the first few months, we were everything: late-night texts, surprise food deliveries, and video call dates. We made promises—of visits, of forever.

But slowly, the time zones got wider. His calls got shorter. My heart got heavier.

I'd ask, "Are we okay?"

He'd say, "You worry too much."

Maybe I did. But I also felt too little—too little effort, too little presence, too much silence.

My birthday came and went with a message that read, "Sorry I missed your call. The meeting ran late."

I didn't cry. I just sat by the window and let the city hum around me, drowning out the sound of what wasn't said.

One day, I met Kabir, a friend who listened. Who made me laugh again. I didn't cheat. But my heart leaned elsewhere, and that scared me more than if I had.

When I told Aarav how lonely I felt, he just stared. And finally said, "Maybe we're trying to hold on to something we already let go of."

We ended softly. No drama. Just truth.

I still miss him. But I don't miss begging for crumbs of connection.

Love came late for me.

I was thirty-six. Divorced. Wiser, maybe. But also guarded. Until Dev entered my life like a question I didn't know I still had.

He was ten years younger. Hindu. I was Muslim.

But more than anything else, he was light—curious, kind, completely unbothered by what people might say. I tried to ignore him. Society had already whispered enough about me—about how I wore my independence too loudly, how I was "too much" for any man.

But Dev didn't whisper. He roared.

He brought me flowers on days I felt like hiding. He held my hand even when relatives stared. And for the first time in years, I let myself feel wanted—not tolerated, not admired—*wanted*.

But then came the harder part.

My mother wouldn't speak to me. His family offered silence coated in politeness. Religion became an elephant in every room we entered.

One night, I asked him, "Will your God and mine ever sit at the same table?"

He didn't answer. He didn't need to.

We weren't just fighting for love. We were fighting to exist in a world where love like ours made people uncomfortable.

The doubts crept in. I wondered if I was being selfish. If he would grow to resent me. If our love was only brave until it became inconvenient.

But he stayed. Not because it was easy—but because walking away would've meant betraying the rarest kind of connection.

In the quiet rebellion of holding each other without apology, we found our prayer.

The three of us met—Aisha, Naina, and I—at a relationship support circle on a sleepy Sunday afternoon, sipping chai and comparing heartaches like battle scars.

Different cities. Different stories.

But the same ache: To be heard. To be chosen. To be loved without translation, without performance, without pain.

We laughed. We cried. We healed.

Aisha taught me that love between cultures isn't a compromise—it's a creation.

Naina reminded me that distance doesn't kill love—neglect does.

And I—Zoya—offered them this: *Sometimes love is your protest. Your prayer. Your power.*

And all of us, in our own ways, discovered this simple truth: When love stops trying to win and starts trying to understand — walls fall. Wounds heal. People soften, and hearts find a home.

Understanding didn't solve every problem. But it became the bridge between silence and safety, between pride and vulnerability, between fear and connection.

If you've ever asked, "Can somebody understand me?"

Know this—Understanding doesn't always come fast. But when it does—it doesn't just change relationships.

It changes lives.

The Long-Distance Strain

Priyanka and Sameer: A Journey from Misunderstanding to Emotional Intimacy

When Priyanka and Sameer first decided to stay together despite living in different cities, they were confident their love could handle it.

Sameer had accepted a demanding but prestigious position with a multinational company in Mumbai, while Priyanka had launched her own freelance design career in Bangalore.

They were both passionate about their work and even more passionate about each other. "Distance makes the heart grow fonder," they had said, laughing and holding hands at the airport when he left. And in the beginning, it did.

Their early days of long-distance were filled with love letters, video calls, surprise deliveries, and shared playlists. Even from miles away, they celebrated small wins together—her first successful project pitch, his promotion to lead strategist, the new café she discovered, and the book he started reading. They made time for each other, no matter how late or early. Even the silences between conversations felt warm.

But slowly, things began to shift.

Their schedules became heavier. Sameer was drowning in back-to-back meetings and outstation presentations. Priyanka's clients had started growing, and so had their expectations. The calls became rushed, and the messages were shorter. Sometimes, they'd go a full day without speaking—and when they finally did, it wasn't the joyful banter of before. It was updates and complaints, a checklist of life rather than the emotional sharing that once defined them.

Priyanka would wait for him to call, keeping her dinner plate aside. She'd look at the clock, hoping the familiar ringtone would ring. When it didn't, frustration would bubble up. One evening, she messaged him, "Busy again?" with a frowning emoji. Sameer, already overwhelmed at work, interpreted it as nagging and shot back, "It's not like I'm on vacation here, Priyanka."

That hurt her more than she expected. She didn't reply.

And so, it began—the silent wars. The cold replies. The sarcastic comments masked as jokes. The small jabs that said, *I'm hurt* but never directly. The more Priyanka reached out emotionally, the more Sameer pulled back, feeling criticized. The more he distanced himself, the more Priyanka felt unloved.

They started to misread each other's intentions. Her need to feel connected came across as insecurity. His silence came across as detachment. They weren't fighting, but they weren't close anymore either. They were drifting—slowly, quietly, painfully.

One evening, during a video call, Priyanka shared a personal story about how she broke down during a pitch meeting after being harshly criticized. She wanted comfort and understanding. But Sameer, multitasking with a report open, barely looked up.

"You need to toughen up, Priyanka. You're too sensitive sometimes," he said casually.

Her eyes welled up. "Do you even hear what I'm saying?" she asked, her voice trembling.

He sighed. "I don't have the energy for this

tonight."

That was the moment she truly broke.

That night, she poured her heart into her journal: *I miss who we were. I miss feeling safe with him. When did love start feeling like walking on eggshells?*

And yet, despite the pain, she didn't want to give up. Not yet.

A few days later, she took a bold step. She sent Sameer a long message—not to accuse him, but to share honestly how she was feeling. She didn't use blame.

She simply wrote: *"I know you're under a lot of pressure. But I feel like I'm losing you, and it's scaring me. I don't want to become strangers who just update each other about work. I want us to still be each other's home. Can we please try again—with more understanding and more honesty?"*

To her surprise, he replied quickly.

"I've been feeling the same. I just didn't know how to say it. Let's talk tonight. Properly. No distractions."

That night, their call lasted four hours. They spoke—really spoke. About the things they had bottled up. About how much they missed each other, about how both were trying in different ways but failing to meet in the middle. They cried. They laughed between tears. It felt like a release.

After that, they began rebuilding.

They created small rituals. Monday night video dinners, Friday morning "just because" voice notes and a weekly letter where they would write about something they appreciated in the other person that week. They didn't wait for special occasions. They celebrated small wins, like Priyanka nailing a challenging design brief or Sameer standing up to his boss for better boundaries.

But the real change wasn't in the schedule. It was in their *attitude*.

They stopped assuming. They started asking.

"Are you okay?" replaced "Why didn't you call?"

"I'm feeling a little distant today—can we talk?" replaced silence.

"I know you didn't mean to hurt me, but..."

replaced "You always…"

With each honest conversation, they stitched the torn fabric of their relationship with threads of empathy.

Sameer began to understand that being present wasn't just about showing up—it was about listening, about feeling what she felt. Priyanka, in turn, realized that love didn't always look like grand gestures—it often looked like a small, consistent effort, even if imperfect.

Months later, when they finally met in person, there was a quiet comfort between them. Not the rush of passion that came with early love—but something deeper. Something earned. A companionship that had been tested, broken, and rebuilt.

They sat in a café one afternoon, fingers interlocked, sipping coffee.

"I was so scared we were going to lose this," Priyanka whispered.

"We almost did," Sameer replied. "But I'm glad we didn't. You taught me that love isn't just about feeling—it's about choosing. Every day."

She smiled. "And understanding. Real, patient, human understanding."

Final Message: In love, effort matters. But *understanding* matters even more. Understanding that your partner isn't perfect, that they have fears they can't name, and days when they fail to show up right—but that they're trying. Understanding that real love is less about grand romance and more about holding space for each other's truths, even the uncomfortable ones.

Understanding that sometimes, the most loving thing we can say is: "I see you. I hear you. And I'm here."

Because, in the end, the greatest distance in any relationship isn't physical. It's emotional disconnection. And the greatest bridge? Its empathy.

Parenting Challenges

Ankit and Sneha – Divergent Views on Discipline

Ankit and Sneha had always envisioned a harmonious family life filled with shared values, laughter, and love. Before becoming parents, they often talked about how they would raise their children—combining discipline and warmth, structure and creativity. But reality, as it often does, turned out to be more complicated than they had imagined.

As parents to their two young children, Aarav and Kiara, they found themselves frequently clashing over their parenting styles. Ankit firmly believed in a strict, structured method of discipline, emphasizing rules, consequences, and a clear sense of authority. He felt this was essential to preparing the children for a competitive, demanding world. "Children need boundaries to thrive," he would say, often reinforcing the importance of respect, responsibility, and accountability.

Sneha, on the other hand, approached parenting with gentleness and empathy. She believed that children are more likely to grow emotionally strong and secure when they are heard and understood. Her parenting philosophy centred around emotional connection, trust, and open communication. She worried that harsh discipline would suppress their children's voices and self-worth. "They'll listen to us when they feel safe with us," she would argue.

Their opposing views quickly became a recurring source of frustration. Whenever Aarav or Kiara misbehaved, the tension escalated—not just between parent and child, but between husband and wife. One such instance was when Aarav refused to complete his homework. Ankit immediately moved to impose a penalty, believing it was necessary to instil discipline. Sneha, however, suggested sitting down and talking with him to understand what was truly going on.

The disagreement escalated into a heated argument.

Ankit, exasperated, would raise his voice, "Can somebody understand me? It's about preparing them for the real world!"

Sneha, her voice trembling with emotion, would reply, "But we need to nurture their hearts first. Fear doesn't build character—love does."

These moments created an emotional distance between them. Their children, sensitive to the household energy, often withdrew or acted out. The home that was meant to be a safe sanctuary began to feel tense and unpredictable. Their parenting conflict was slowly becoming a relationship conflict.

Everything began to change when they decided to attend a parenting workshop together—partly out of desperation and partly because, deep down, they still believed in each other.

The workshop facilitator introduced the idea that discipline and empathy are not opposites—they can co-exist. Through guided activities and reflective sessions, Ankit and Sneha began to uncover the roots of their parenting beliefs. Ankit realized that his strict nature stemmed from his childhood under authoritarian parents. On the other hand, Sneha had grown up in a house that emphasized emotional freedom but lacked structure—and she had often felt lost without boundaries.

They saw, perhaps for the first time, that their differing approaches were not about "right vs wrong" but about "past vs present." Their parenting styles were shaped by their inner wounds. This realization shifted something deep within them.

Together, they began crafting a new approach—one that blended the best of both worlds. They agreed to create a calm, emotionally safe environment where expectations were clear, consequences were fair, and love was always unconditional.

They also made a powerful decision: to stop arguing in front of the children. They chose to walk the talk—modelling respect, collaboration, and emotional maturity through their actions, not just their words. They promised each other never to make fake promises to the children and to lead with integrity.

They created a weekly ritual—an hour every Sunday night—to sit together and reflect on parenting challenges. During one such meeting, they decided that whenever a conflict arose with the children, they would first understand the emotions involved and only then talk about the consequences.

For instance, when Aarav began showing defiance at school, they invited him to a "family circle" instead of immediately punishing him. He tearfully shared that he felt invisible whenever his achievements weren't as celebrated as Kiara's. It was a revelation that changed everything. Ankit hugged him tightly and whispered, "I'm proud of you, always." That moment healed more than just a behavioural issue—it healed a part of Aarav's heart.

As this new dynamic took root, their home changed. It became warmer, calmer, and more harmonious. The children began to respond positively, not out of fear, but from genuine understanding and connection. Aarav became more confident and emotionally expressive. Kiara, once shy and moody, began showing remarkable leadership at school, organizing art events and helping younger kids feel included.

Years passed.

Aarav grew up to become a respected child counsellor, often using stories from his own upbringing to help young clients and their parents reconnect. "My dad used to be strict," he once told a teenage boy, "But he chose to listen—and that changed me." He was deeply empathetic, and his ability to connect with troubled kids was extraordinary.

Kiara, equally brilliant, found her calling in creative leadership. In her acclaimed TED Talk *"Creativity in Calm,"* she said, "My parents didn't give me a perfect childhood—they gave me a safe one. That's where all my ideas were born." The audience rose in applause, but in the front row, Sneha wiped silent tears as Ankit squeezed her hand, overwhelmed with quiet pride.

Even in everyday moments, the impact of their parenting was visible. Aarav once gently consoled his niece during a tantrum, kneeling down to her level and asking, "Are you feeling unheard or just tired?" Kiara advocated for mental health days at her workplace, saying, "My mom always told me rest is strength, not weakness."

Their children's success wasn't just in titles or applause—it was in who they had become: kind, aware, resilient, and emotionally intelligent human beings.

As Ankit and Sneha sat together one quiet evening, sipping tea on their balcony, they reflected on the years gone by. The house echoed with the distant laughter of their now-grown children. Sneha leaned her head on Ankit's shoulder, and he softly said, "We did okay, didn't we?" She smiled, eyes misty, "We did better than okay—we healed while parenting. That was the real gift."

They didn't just raise children. They raised a home built on trust. They raised a generation capable of loving, listening, and leading with heart. They raised a legacy.

And in that knowing, their hearts were full.

The Neighbourhood Ties

Neeta had always been the heartbeat of the neighbourhood — vibrant, expressive, and unapologetically alive. Festivals were her playground, a canvas where she painted joy with music, lights, and laughter. Her apartment lit up like a dream during Diwali, echoing with celebration.

It wasn't just a party—it was tradition, memory, and identity, all wrapped into one glowing evening.

Living next door was Aditi—a quieter soul who was gentle and observant and recently moved in with her husband and twin toddlers. For her, life had become a pattern of routines and exhaustion. Motherhood had embraced her like a tidal wave—beautiful but overwhelming. Nights were sleepless, days were long, and every little thing needed attention.

She had no problem with joy—just hoped it came with a bit of thoughtfulness.

Their worlds collided one Diwali evening.

That day, Neeta was in full festive mode. Rangoli adorned her entrance, strings of marigolds swayed from the balcony, and upbeat music played in the background. Children laughed, firecrackers burst rhythmically, and relatives flowed in and out of her house with smiles and sweets.

Aditi had just gotten her twins to sleep after nearly two hours of rocking and lullabies. Her husband, exhausted from a long hospital shift, was asleep in the other room. For a rare moment, there was calm.

Then came the burst—first a string of firecrackers, then loud music from Neeta's balcony.

One child woke up screaming. Then the other.

Her husband stirred, groaned, and turned to the wall.

Tired, desperate, and still carrying one baby, Aditi stepped out and knocked on Neeta's door.

Neeta, mid-celebration, opened it—her face glowing, smile wide—only for her expression to stiffen at Aditi's words:

"Can you please tone it down? The kids haven't slept, and it's really too much."

There was silence.

A polite nod.

And a door quietly shut.

From that moment, something invisible shifted.

Neeta felt attacked on her favourite day of the year, misunderstood in the one space she felt most herself. Aditi felt dismissed—made to feel like a burden for asking for peace.

Over the following weeks, the two women continued their routines. They crossed paths in elevators, hallways, and balconies—but with silence instead of smiles.

They both wanted to move past it. Yet pride and uncertainty held them back. Each believed she had only asked for what was fair.

Aditi questioned herself often—Had I been rude? Should I have waited? Was wanting quiet for my children too much?

Neeta, on the other hand, wrestled with the sting of being judged — Did she not see how much love and effort went into that celebration? Did she only see noise?

Neither knew how to bridge the gap.

Things didn't improve quickly. A week after Diwali, Aditi had ordered a box of groceries, and the delivery guy rang Neeta's doorbell by mistake. Neeta opened the door, found the box, and, with a brief, cold knock, handed it to Aditi without a word. Aditi, still holding her baby in one arm, thanked her, but Neeta had already turned away.

Another day, Aditi tried to greet Neeta's dog, Mishti, on the staircase. Mishti, the cheerful beagle, wagged her tail and tried jumping toward Aditi. But Neeta quickly tugged the leash and walked ahead. Aditi stood frozen for a moment, feeling like a stranger in her own corridor.

The tension became visible. Even neighbours noticed it—some whispered, others shrugged. But the air remained thick.

Then, one day, as fate would have it, Aditi's son fell while playing in the society garden. He scraped his knee badly and began crying uncontrollably. Aditi, who had just stepped away to take a phone call, came rushing. And to her surprise, she saw Neeta already beside him, gently wiping the wound with tissues from her purse and whispering stories about brave lions who didn't cry.

Aditi slowed her pace as she approached. Her son, still sniffling, clutched the chocolate Neeta had given him.

"He's a brave one," Neeta said softly, without looking up.

Aditi crouched down beside her. "Thank you... for being there."

"We've all been there."

That night, Aditi sat on her balcony. Across the railing, Neeta stood watering her plants. For the first time in weeks, their eyes met and lingered. A moment passed. Aditi raised her hand slightly. Neeta nodded in return.

Then came Holi.

The society planned a terrace potluck—simple, peaceful, just lights, food, and soft conversations.

Aditi hadn't planned on going. But when her daughter tugged her hand and whispered, "Mumma… go up? Lights?" she couldn't say no.

She reached the terrace in a simple Kurti, holding her daughter.

And there stood Neeta—arranging paper lanterns with the elderly Mrs. Sharma, her saree fluttering in the wind. Their eyes met.

A moment. A pause. A walk across the terrace.

"Hi," Neeta said gently.

"Hi," Aditi replied, adjusting her daughter's dupatta.

"She's grown so much," Neeta said.

"She talks now," Aditi smiled. "And argues like a lawyer."

Neeta chuckled.

Then, softly— "That night… during Diwali… I think I was too caught up. I didn't try to see your side. I'm sorry."

Aditi blinked, surprised.

"I wasn't kind either," she replied. "I was drained and didn't think about what Diwali meant to you. I'm sorry, too."

Neeta smiled. "Maybe we forgot, for a minute, that we weren't just neighbours. We were women living next to each other's worlds."

Aditi looked up at the lanterns swaying above. "Seems silly now, doesn't it?"

"Not silly," Neeta said. "Just human."

The baby reached out toward the glowing lanterns. Neeta pulled out a small pink one from her bag. "Here. For her. Let it be the first lantern between us."

Aditi took it gently. "Thank you."

In the distance, someone began playing a soft song. Neeta pointed toward the food. "Come. There's jalebi." Aditi laughed. "That's one language I always understand."

And just like that, the silence was broken.

Not by noise, but by kindness.

By words left unspoken for too long.

By two women finally seeing each other—not as a nuisance or an obstacle—but as neighbours, mothers, women, and most importantly, as human beings.

A single lantern now glowed between them.

And the question that once echoed in both their hearts— "Can somebody understand me?"—had finally found its answer.

Retirement After Being Alone: Mr. Uday's Journey of Rediscovery

Mr. Uday sat in his favourite chair by the window, watching the sun dip beneath the horizon. The golden light cast a soft glow on his face, reflecting the wisdom and peace that had come to define his life in these later years. At 80, life had taken many turns, but it was in these final chapters that he found the truest meaning of living.

After the passing of his beloved wife, Seema, Mr. Uday felt a deep emptiness. The house, once filled with laughter and love, became eerily quiet. Grief consumed him, and with it came an unexpected shift in his temperament. He became irritable, snapping at his children and grandchildren over the smallest things. His heart ached for Seema's presence. Without her, he struggled to find a sense of purpose. His world had been shaken, and in his pain, he began to feel neglected—as though no one truly understood him.

He grew rigid, clinging to old routines and rules, believing they were the only way to maintain control in a now unpredictable world. His fixed mindset intensified, and he began imposing his way of life onto those around him. He expected his children to live by his standards, convinced that discipline and order were the only answers to his inner chaos. But no matter how hard he tried, things weren't the same. A part of him longed for the warmth of the past—the comfort of Seema's love and the deep bond they had shared.

Mr. Uday's frustration grew. Every day felt like a battle. He criticized his children's choices, believing they were too modern and carefree. He judged his grandchildren for their lack of respect for tradition, and slowly, his family began to distance themselves. He felt invisible—his voice fading in his own home. He believed no one understood his pain, and in that isolation, he withdrew further.

It was his 10-year-old granddaughter, Riya, who first opened his eyes. With a carefree spirit and an open heart, she walked up to him one afternoon while he was lost in thought.

"Grandpa, I made something for you!" she said brightly, holding a sketchbook.

He accepted it, expecting playful doodles. But as he opened the pages, he was taken aback. They were filled with vibrant colours—sketches of landscapes and portraits. Riya had a natural gift for art, something he had never noticed. One drawing struck him most: a portrait of himself as a younger man, smiling joyfully with Seema at his side.

He stared at it for a long time. The memory of Seema filled his heart—but more than that, Riya had captured a moment of happiness, a reminder that life had been full of love and connection, not just rules and expectations.

That evening, something shifted. As he sat with his family, he didn't feel the need to correct or impose. For the first time in years, he was simply present—not as a father trying to teach or a grandfather setting an example—but as a man embracing the changing tides of life.

In the months that followed, Mr. Uday began to change in ways he never imagined. He took up new hobbies, breaking free from his strict routines. He began painting—something he had always wanted to try but had never made time for. It wasn't about creating masterpieces—it was about expressing himself, finding joy in mixing colours, and watching blank canvases come to life.

Art gave him a voice when words failed. He painted landscapes, portraits, and abstract reflections of his emotions. But, he longed to share his work and connect with others through his art.

Riya, ever curious and tech-savvy, noticed his growing collection.

"Grandpa, why don't you share your paintings online?" she suggested. "You might even get noticed!"

He hesitated. Social media was unfamiliar territory. But Riya patiently guided him, helping him set up an account, upload his artwork, and write captions that captured his feelings.

"Let your art speak for itself," she said, beaming.

To his surprise, people began to respond. Viewers praised the emotional depth of his work. Comments poured in from strangers who felt touched by his story and art. Encouraged by Riya, Mr. Uday began selling his paintings. What began as a healing hobby became a passion—and then, a bridge connecting him to the world.

As his online following grew, so did his confidence. He received messages from people around the world thanking him for his vulnerability and creativity. His art was featured in online galleries, and commission requests started to come in. The recognition was humbling—but more than that, it gave him a renewed sense of purpose.

One evening, while strolling through his feed with his family, his son Raj said, "Dad, I can't believe how much you've accomplished. This is amazing."

Mr. Uday smiled, his heart full. "It's not about fame or money. It's about finding joy again. It's about living with an open heart."

He no longer obsessed over his children's choices or how they lived. He realized that his discipline had been a shield—a way to cope with grief. But now, he saw that love and understanding were far more powerful. He wasn't afraid to be vulnerable. He embraced change and let life unfold without trying to control it.

In quiet moments, he reflected on his journey. Losing Seema was the hardest chapter of his life—but it was also the beginning of his transformation.

Through pain, he rediscovered himself. He learned that happiness doesn't come from controlling or making others follow your ways. It comes from acceptance—of life, of people, and of oneself.

Surrounded by laughter and love, Mr. Uday realized the key to a fulfilling life: **understanding each other, offering compassion, and embracing change with an open heart**.

He had gone from feeling invisible to being deeply seen—because he had chosen to understand others and, more importantly, to understand himself.

Moral of the Story:

The story of Mr. Uday reminds us that understanding others begins with understanding ourselves. When we become rigid and stuck in our ways, we often feel misunderstood and neglected. But when we open our hearts, embrace change, and let go of unnecessary expectations, we create space for meaningful connections.

By seeing the world through others' eyes and pursuing our passions with vulnerability and openness, we not only heal ourselves but also foster deeper harmony with those around us.

The Turning Point – A Journey to Understanding

Anil Deshmukh sat by the window, as he did every morning, watching the world move on while something inside him remained stuck. The street outside his Nashik home was alive with its usual rhythm—bicycle bells, chai stalls, distant temple bells—but within his heart, there was only the slow silence of age, restlessness, and a growing disconnection from the life he once thought he controlled. At fifty, retired from the Indian Railways, Anil had everything he had worked for—financial stability, a home, a pension. And yet, peace remained elusive.

His morning rituals were heavy with habit: chai, two cigarettes, a newspaper read from front to back, and muttered judgments about today's generation. By evening, he would pour himself two drinks—"just to relax," he told himself. But the truth was, the drink and the smoke weren't indulgences anymore. They were crutches. He had started relying on them to fill a void he didn't know how to name.

His son Kaival, once his shadow, had now become a distant blur. Once inseparable—building model trains, riding scooters, telling stories—now, their conversations had narrowed to silence and sighs. Kaival, now 24, had chosen to pursue photography, rejecting the engineering job Anil had arranged through old contacts. That decision sparked one of the many fights between them, ending with words neither wanted to say and a door that was slammed harder than necessary.

"He doesn't respect me anymore," Anil told himself. But deep down, he knew—he didn't understand him anymore. And maybe he never really tried to.

Meanwhile, in Ahmedabad, Kavita Shah adjusted the pleats of a mannequin in her boutique, but her mind wasn't in it. At 46, Kavita had built a business she was once proud of—a traditional boutique filled with carefully curated ethnic wear. It had once thrived with walk-in customers, word-of-mouth sales, and neighbourhood admiration. But now, footfall had slowed. Trends were digital, fashion was faster, and young clients no longer found her designs "relevant."

She knew what the problem was: she had fallen behind. Not because she lacked talent but because she was afraid—afraid of change, of technology, of being ridiculed. Her daughter Isha, a social media-savvy mental health content creator, often encouraged her: "Ma, let's shoot a reel. Let me show you how easy it is." Kavita always replied softly but stubbornly, "Not now, beta." But it was never about time. It was about fear.

She had also developed a new routine she never spoke about—hours of scrolling through reels, watching daily soaps she didn't even enjoy, and playing meaningless mobile games into the night. "I'm just relaxing," she would tell herself. But she wasn't relaxing. She was escaping—from her fading relevance, her fear of failure, and a growing emptiness she didn't know how to confront.

Anil, too, was spiralling in his own way. He had tried quitting his vices multiple times. He had gone to temples, touched the cold marble floor with his forehead, and taken vows. "No more smoking. No more drinking," he whispered to Lord Shiva, only to light another cigarette four hours later. The cycle repeated endlessly—promises made in guilt, broken in silence. The first puff, the first sip—always followed by shame, then surrender.

What he didn't realize was that it wasn't just nicotine or alcohol he was addicted to—it was avoidance. The drinks numbed the ache of an empty home, the cigarettes dulled the sharpness of his son's absence, and the rituals masked the truth he wasn't ready to face: he had lost touch not just with Kaival but with himself.

Everything changed the morning he collapsed while picking up the newspaper. It wasn't a heart attack, but the doctors warned, "Your lungs are deteriorating. Your liver is under strain. You have to stop." That evening, instead of lighting a cigarette, he lit a diya. But the cravings came back, intense and uncontrollable. He poured half a drink, then dumped it into the sink. But an hour later, he poured another and finished it quietly on the terrace.

He cried that night. The turning point came in the most unexpected way. A retired colleague spoke to him about chakra healing. "It's not magic," the man said. "It's awareness. It helps you look at the pain you've buried."

With nothing left to lose, Anil tried a guided meditation. It was a simple heart chakra practice. He closed his eyes and listened. As the calm voice spoke of compassion and forgiveness, memories surfaced—Kaival as a child, his laughter, his drawings, the sound of his footsteps running down the hall. The pain came like a wave, and so did the tears.

He began doing it daily. Focused breathing. Gentle music. Chakra affirmations. Especially the solar plexus for inner strength and the throat chakra for the words he never said. He also began journaling his urges. "What am I feeling when I want to smoke? What pain am I trying to drink away?" He still slipped. Still smoked on difficult days. But now, he didn't lie to himself about it. He faced it. And that made all the difference.

Kavita's shift came more subtly. One evening, she missed a client appointment because she was too engrossed in a reel series. Her assistant said, "Madam, you've changed these days." The words stung. That night, her mobile battery died, and she stared at her reflection on the black screen. Puffy eyes. Tired skin. A woman who had once dreamed of her name on a boutique board was now addicted to games and TV serials.

The next morning, she opened the journal Isha had given her months ago. She wrote a single line: "I am afraid of being left behind." Then more: "I am afraid my time has passed. I am afraid I'm no longer needed." And beneath those words came something softer: "But maybe I can begin again."

She deleted the games. Blocked her social media for a week. She sat down at her design table with a piece of raw cotton and a sketch pencil. Her fingers hesitated, then flowed. The lines weren't perfect, but they were real.

A few days later, she looked at Isha and said, "Will you teach me how to shoot a reel?" Isha's eyes lit up. "Are you serious?" Kavita smiled shyly. "Let's try."

They filmed together. The first one was clumsy, unedited, and utterly honest. The feedback was overwhelmingly positive. "You remind me of my mother." "This is so wholesome." "Never too late to start." Kavita didn't care about going viral. She had gone visible—in her own eyes.

Anil, inspired by his healing, messaged Kaival: "I want to understand your world. Will you show it to me?" The video calls that followed were awkward at first. But Kaival showed him his work. Portraits of street vendors, rickshaw drivers, old hands, and weathered faces. "They're invisible to most people," Kaival said. "But I see them. And I want the world to see them, too."

Anil didn't fully understand the art. But he understood the intention. The compassion. And for the first time, he saw his son not as a boy who rejected structure but as a man who embraced empathy. They began speaking more often—sometimes about photography, sometimes about trains, sometimes just about life.

Anil started sketching again—locomotives, landscapes, even a few portraits. Kaival printed one of his father's sketches and framed it in his studio with a caption: "The journey back is the most courageous of all." Anil quit smoking completely two months later. The drinks became rare. The craving faded—not by force, but by love.

Kavita rebranded her boutique *Revive – Designs for the Soul.* Each piece came with a handwritten note: "Created with heart, from a woman who remembered herself." Younger customers started coming in. But more importantly, she came back to herself.

The transformation wasn't perfect. They still had off days. Still felt the pull of old habits. But they now had tools—awareness, breath, honesty, and understanding. Understanding of themselves, of their children, and of the silent pain that had lived inside them for years.

In the end, the real turning point wasn't a dramatic gesture. It was the quiet decision to stop running. To sit with the discomfort. To listen. To change—not for anyone else, but for their own peace.

Because the greatest healing doesn't come from control, it comes from **connection.**

With the self.

With the ones we love.

And with the truth, we are finally ready to face.

The Soul Who Was Finally... Understood

Aryan Kapoor, 32, was a name that echoed in boardrooms and financial circles across the country. The youngest CEO of one of the nation's largest mutual fund houses, he was hailed as a visionary and a genius in investment strategy. Headlines called him "The Wizard of Wealth," and corporate honchos envied his meteoric rise.

But behind the tailored suits and billion-dollar decisions lived a man who was once very different.

Aryan's childhood was cocooned in luxury—expensive toys, elite schools, lavish vacations. He was a polite, shy, happy-go-lucky boy who loved music, believed in kindness, and dreamed simple dreams. Life was golden until it wasn't. A business crisis brought his father's empire crumbling down. Yet even in financial ruin, his father preserved Aryan's education with dignity, planting deep roots of resilience in his heart.

That struggle carved Aryan's character. He worked hard, studied harder, and eventually built his empire from scratch. Success didn't come easy, but it came big.

And so did **Sambhavi**—his life partner.

Sambhavi was born into wealth, educated at top international institutions, and possessed a mind as sharp as it was compassionate. She could've led global ventures or headed her own conglomerate, but she made a quiet, powerful choice—to be a homemaker, not out of compulsion but out of conviction. She dreamt of building a home filled with love, shared meals, children's laughter, and emotional grounding—a space where Aryan could return and find peace beyond power.

Together, they had a son, Vivaan—a mirror of Aryan's younger self, full of spark and wonder.

But as Aryan's professional world grew taller, the walls around his personal life thickened. Late-night meetings turned into lonely hotel rooms. A glass of wine became a silent companion. The vibrant man Sambhavi fell in love with faded into a figure constantly stressed, irritated, and disconnected. His laugh vanished. His conversations became transactional. His presence at home was more physical than emotional.

The health warnings came early—high blood pressure, early diabetes, mental fog—but he dismissed them. At home, frustration replaced affection. He'd snap at small things, forget promises made, and rarely looked present, even when he was physically there.

"No one cares about me!"

"You're all here for my money!"

"No one understands me!"

At one point, after repeated emotional breakdowns at home and pressure from family and even his own father, Aryan made an effort. For a few weeks, he tried to be more involved with Vivaan, sat at the dining table more regularly, and even scheduled a family outing or two. Sambhavi noticed—his effort was there, but his presence... wasn't.

Even during family dinners, he would suddenly stand up mid-meal and walk out of the room to take client calls that lasted an hour. Sometimes, he'd return and forget they were in the middle of dinner. He forgot what he had said minutes earlier or what Vivaan had just asked him. His unpredictability became unsettling.

Vivaan once whispered to Sambhavi, "Is Papa sick in the heart?"

It broke her.

Aryan, meanwhile, was drowning—and didn't even know it. Somewhere deep inside, he began blaming others—particularly his parents. He remembered the arguments he had witnessed between his mother and father as a child. Harsh words, cold silences, slammed doors. The emotional discomfort had left a scar he never addressed.

One night, overwhelmed and intoxicated, Aryan snapped at Sambhavi, "I was never meant for a peaceful life... maybe it's in my blood. My parents fought all the time! Maybe that's why I turned out this way!"

His words echoed in the stillness of the room.

The next morning, his father, now in his late sixties but still carrying a quiet strength, asked to speak with him privately.

They sat on the terrace, where the breeze carried years of memory.

His father spoke softly, "Aryan, I heard what you said last night... and it broke my heart."

Aryan looked away, silent.

"I won't deny it—we fought. Yes, your mother and I argued often. We were both stubborn and strong-willed. Life tested us... loss, debt, ego, exhaustion. But behind every fight was love. We never stopped caring—even when we couldn't express it right."

He paused, then looked straight at Aryan.

"Do you know how many nights I stayed awake worrying about your future? How many times your mother hid her tears to protect your innocence? We weren't perfect, son. But we were real. And we never gave up on each other. That's how we survived. That's how *you* had the strength to rise again after I lost everything."

"Your habits, your choices—don't put them on our shoulders. You are not a prisoner of our past, Aryan. You're free to write your own story. And I promise you... it can still be beautiful."

Aryan's eyes filled. At that moment, something clicked inside him. The anger, the blame—it began to dissolve.

And then came **Naina**, an unexpected guest from the past.

Aryan met her at a finance summit. Once the star of their college, Naina was still the same—poised, intelligent, and emotionally intuitive. She instantly sensed something off in Aryan. "You, okay?" she asked, her tone simple but sincere. "You look... tired. Not just outside. In here," she said, lightly touching her chest.

Aryan, for the first time in a long while, didn't pretend. He let himself speak.

Naina reached out again. And again. Slowly, conversations turned into realizations. When she met Sambhavi, a bond formed almost instantly—two women, different in their journeys but united in their love and concern for the same man.

They didn't push Aryan. They just *showed up*.

Sambhavi began reintroducing the forgotten rhythm of the family—evening tea, candle-lit dinners, and small celebrations of ordinary days. Naina nudged Aryan toward mindfulness—journaling, meditating, even nature walks. He resisted, of course. Change hurts before it heals.

But healing did come.

One evening, Aryan came home early. Vivaan ran to him, beaming, holding a crayon-streaked card that said, *"I miss old Papa."*

His hands trembled. His breath caught.

He walked into the kitchen, where Sambhavi was humming to herself and chopping vegetables. Her face lit up when she saw him, but she stayed silent, sensing the storm within him.

He broke. His voice cracked. "I don't want to be this man anymore…"

Sambhavi walked to him and gently cupped his face. Her words were soft, but they carried the weight of a thousand quiet heartbreaks.

"Aryan… listen to me. I never married your success. I never fell in love with your designations, your suits, or the numbers in your bank account.

I fell in love with the boy who stayed up late solving his father's problems without losing hope… the man who once danced in the kitchen with me in his pajamas, who cried when Vivaan was born, who held my hand like it was the only thing that mattered.

That's the man I married. That's the man I still see—somewhere behind all this exhaustion and pain. And yes, right now, you're broken. But even in your brokenness, I believe in you. Not because you're perfect but because you have the courage to face your imperfections.

I didn't sign up for an easy life, Aryan... I signed up for a real one. With you. Always with you."

He crumbled into her arms.

That night, something in Aryan shifted. Not all at once—but enough.

In the weeks that followed, Aryan did more than just adjust his routine—he redesigned his life.

He appointed a capable second-in-command to manage daily operations. He stopped taking work calls after 7 PM. And finally, after years, he planned a **long family vacation to Switzerland**—Sambhavi's dream destination.

No business calls. No meetings. Just snowflakes, mountains, warm cocoa, and laughter.

For the first time in years, Aryan watched Vivaan build a snowman, laughed with Sambhavi under the stars, and sat silently beside his parents sipping coffee—with no devices, no distractions, no deadlines.

In the beginning, detaching from his work felt strange. His fingers twitched for his phone; his mind drifted toward markets. But slowly, he began to breathe differently. *Live* differently. And eventually, this new rhythm became second nature.

He made weekends sacred—reserved only for family. His health reports came back normal. His face looked younger. Lighter.

And one evening, as they strolled by Lake Geneva, Sambhavi stopped, looked at him, her eyes glistening with quiet joy, and whispered,

"Thank you, Aryan... for giving me my dream husband back."

Aryan smiled—not the forced smile he wore at corporate events, but the one that reached his eyes, the one that once made Sambhavi fall in love.

The home was no longer a battlefield. It became a sanctuary.

And as for Aryan, he didn't just reclaim his happiness—he *remembered* who he truly was. The boy who believed in love. The man who chose family. The son who now understood his parents. The husband who became his wife's dream. The father who showed up.

The soul who was finally... understood.

Take Away from the Stories:

Who should understand whom?

The true takeaway from this heartfelt story is that in every relationship—especially between parents and children—the deepest need isn't control or constant connection but the reassurance that *somebody understands me.* When parents loosen their grip and allow their children the space to grow, they foster not distance but trust. And when children recognize that behind their parents' expectations lies a heart full of care, the emotional bond deepens. The river of love flows best when it's not forced into a direction but allowed its natural course. In the end, all anyone really wants is to feel that in this vast, often overwhelming world, *somebody understands me—* without judgment, pressure, or expectations.

Anything Will Do: A Story of Love, Misunderstandings, and Understanding

One of the most powerful takeaways from this story is the deep human need to feel seen, heard, and understood. At its core, Ketki wasn't asking *what* to cook—she was really saying, *"Somebody understands me. Somebody notices that I'm trying."* And Tarun, in his silence, was saying, *"Somebody understands how tired I am. Somebody sees that I'm struggling too."* In every relationship, beneath the surface of daily routines and small questions lies a silent plea: *"Somebody understands me."* This story reminds us that love isn't about agreeing on everything or being perfect partners—it's about showing up, paying attention, and recognizing each other's silent emotions. Because the smallest gesture, when it carries understanding, can heal even the deepest distances.

Preksha – Finally, Somebody Understood Me

The core takeaway from *"Preksha – Finally, Somebody Understood Me"* is that true happiness doesn't come from external validation but from reconnecting with oneself and being seen for who you truly are. Preksha's journey reflects the silent cries of many women who give everything to their families but feel emotionally invisible. The turning point in her life wasn't just when she found fame on social media or when people praised her beauty—it was when she finally whispered in her heart, "Somebody understands me," and that 'somebody' was first herself. The real transformation began the moment she chose to stop seeking love in the wrong places and instead nurtured the love within. Only then could Piyush, her husband, truly see her soul and understand her in a way that mattered. This story reminds us that every individual longs not just to be loved but to be *understood*, and when that happens—when somebody truly understands us—we begin to bloom.

A Newly Married Couple – How Love Survived the Storm of Misunderstanding

The heart of this story lies in the quiet yet powerful realization that love isn't just about grand gestures—it's about presence, patience, and the willingness to truly understand one another. When Pranav and Pankti drifted apart, it wasn't because they stopped loving each other—it was because they stopped showing up emotionally. But through empathy, effort, and honest communication, they found their way back. In their journey, what mattered most was not just being heard but being felt—when Pankti looked at Pranav and finally felt, *"Somebody understands me."* And when Pranav, lost in the chaos of daily life, felt the warmth of her silent support, he too realized, *"Somebody understands me."* That simple, profound feeling—of being seen, heard, and accepted—is what healed their relationship and made their love stronger than ever.

Garbh Sanskar: The First Embrace

The heartfelt takeaway from this story is that every soul longs to be understood—even before birth. Through *Garbh Sanskar*, Mira and Aarav didn't just prepare for their child physically; they opened a sacred space where their baby's soul could whisper, "Somebody understands me." This understanding wasn't born out of instruction but out of intention—through music, quiet conversations, mindful moments, and deep emotional presence. The story teaches us that when we slow down, listen, and love with awareness, we don't just raise children—we nurture souls who feel safe, seen, and deeply connected. It's a reminder to every parent and every human being: understanding begins long before words, and sometimes, the most powerful thing we can offer is our stillness, our attention, and our unconditional embrace.

Employer–Employee: The Power of Mutual Understanding

The key takeaway from Sujay's story is simple yet profound: when leaders choose to listen, understand, and truly care, transformation follows—both in people and performance. This story is a reminder that employees are not just numbers on a spreadsheet; they are human beings with emotions, struggles, and dreams. Sujay's decision to prioritize emotional well-being over rigid performance metrics created a culture shift—one where people felt safe, valued, and heard. The moment his team began to feel, *"Somebody finally understands me,"* everything changed. Productivity soared not because of pressure but because of purpose. Loyalty deepened, not out of obligation, but from connection. In a world that often forgets the human side of business, this story reinforces a timeless truth: understanding is the foundation of all great leadership.

Understanding the Unseen: One Woman's Truth Beyond Poverty

The true takeaway from Mira's story is that everyone, no matter how quiet or unseen, carries a world within them—a world of struggles, dreams, and unspoken strength. Mira's journey reminds us that dignity does not depend on wealth, and integrity isn't tied to status. For years, she moved through life unnoticed beyond her duties—until one moment of crisis revealed the depth of her character. It wasn't the necklace or even the hospital moment that changed everything—it was the realization in Mrs. Roy's eyes, that day in the hospital, when she whispered with tears, *"You could've walked away... but you didn't."* And Mira's gentle reply, *"I didn't forget who I am."* That was the moment the world seemed to say to Mira, *"Finally, somebody understands me."* Not for her work but for her worth. Not for her sacrifice but for her soul.

Friends in the Crossfire: *A story of unspoken truths, quiet resilience, and love beyond labels*

At its heart, *Friends in the Crossfire* is a quiet, powerful reminder of what it means to be truly understood. Sameera and Vikram's story isn't about grand gestures or dramatic love—it's about the rare, sacred comfort of knowing that *somebody understands me.* In a world where people often hide their pain behind smiles and success, this story shows how deep connection thrives not in fixing each other but in *holding space* for one another. When Sameera lights a diya for Vikram, and he folds her father's shawl into her hands, those moments speak louder than a thousand words. It tells us that being understood isn't always about talking more—it's about being seen, felt, and gently held through life's silent battles.

Generational Gaps: Grandfather and Anaya: A Clash of Values

At the heart of this story lies a universal yearning—to be seen, heard, and understood. *"Somebody understands me"* becomes more than a cry for empathy; it transforms into a bridge that connects generations. Through the evolving bond between Grandfather and Anaya, we see that true understanding doesn't require agreement but open-hearted listening and respect. The story reminds us that differences in values, lifestyle, or beliefs need not divide us. Instead, when we pause to truly engage with each other's worlds, we discover that love can hold space for both tradition and individuality. In a world often fragmented by change, the most powerful healing comes from the moment when someone finally says, *"Now I see you. Somebody understands me."*

The Workplace Dilemma: Rohan and Priya – Navigating Power Dynamics

The core takeaway from *"The Workplace Dilemma: Rohan and Priya – Navigating Power Dynamics"* is the transformative power of being truly seen and heard in a professional setting. Priya carried the weight of expectations silently, believing that resilience meant endurance without complaint. But what she truly needed wasn't just recognition for her work—it was acknowledgment of her humanity. When Rohan finally said, *"I'd really like to understand where I went wrong,"* it wasn't just a manager seeking feedback; it was a person reaching out. At that moment, Priya felt something shift inside her—a quiet but profound feeling: *somebody understands me.* That understanding became the turning point, proving that emotional connection, even in high-performance environments, can rebuild trust, restore morale, and ultimately create healthier, more empathetic teams.

The Art of Being Siblings

A Story of Rivalry, Realization, and Reconnection

"The Art of Being Siblings" reminds us that behind every rivalry lies a quiet longing—to be seen, valued, and understood. Neha and Karan's story isn't just about competition; it's about the ache of invisibility, even within a loving family. The turning point doesn't come with grand apologies but in those powerful, vulnerable moments where both siblings whisper in their own way: *"I wish someone understood me."* And in finally hearing each other, they discover that love isn't just about praise or success—it's about presence. When a family begins to truly listen, the words *"somebody understands me"* no longer sound like a desperate plea but a comforting truth.

Across Borders, Between Hearts

This story is a quiet anthem for every heart that's ever whispered, *"I just want somebody to understand me."* It reminds us that love isn't just about fireworks or eternal promises—it's about the everyday effort to bridge differences, listen without defence, and honour each other's roots. Whether it's Aisha navigating cultural expectations, Naina enduring the silence of distance, or Zoya challenging the weight of societal judgment, each woman's journey leads to the same truth: true connection begins not with being right but with being real. When someone finally says, "I see you, I hear you, you're not too much,"—that's when love becomes safe enough to stay. That's when *somebody understands me,* and it becomes not just a hope but a reality.

The Long-Distance Strain

Priyanka and Sameer: A Journey from Misunderstanding to Emotional Intimacy

At its core, *Priyanka and Sameer's* story is a powerful reminder that love isn't just about presence— it's about presence with understanding. What saved their relationship wasn't grand gestures but the quiet, courageous act of saying, "I miss you," and truly listening when the other said, "I'm hurting." The turning point came when Priyanka chose honesty over silence, expressing her feelings without blame, and Sameer responded not with defence but with vulnerability. At that moment, the emotional wall between them began to crumble. For both of them, it wasn't just about being loved—it was about feeling, "Finally, somebody understands me." That sense of being seen and heard became the foundation for rebuilding their intimacy. In love, the deepest healing happens not when everything is perfect but when we say the imperfect out loud and find that the other person stays.

Parenting Challenges

Ankit and Sneha – Divergent Views on Discipline

At its heart, *Ankit and Sneha – Divergent Views on Discipline* is a story about learning to truly understand—not just our children but also each other as partners. It reminds us that parenting is not about perfection but about presence, empathy, and growth. The moment Ankit realized that his need for structure was rooted in his own childhood and Sneha saw how her gentleness was shaped by her past, something shifted—they no longer argued to win but to understand. That turning point—when they looked at each other during the workshop and silently said, *"Somebody understands me now"*—became the foundation of a new way of parenting and loving. It's a powerful reminder that healing begins when we feel truly seen and that children thrive when the adults in their lives choose connection over control.

The Neighbourhood Ties

"The Neighbourhood Ties" is a tender reminder that behind every closed door is a story, a struggle, a longing to be seen. Through the journey of Neeta and Aditi—two women separated by noise, fatigue, and unspoken emotions—the story gently unravels how misunderstandings can harden hearts, but small acts of empathy can soften them again. In a world where everyone is carrying something, the need to be understood—to be truly seen without judgment—is universal. When Neeta and Aditi finally acknowledged each other's realities, the silence between them wasn't filled with noise but with recognition. In that shared moment, what they both longed for quietly unfolded: *"Somebody understands me."* It wasn't about who was right or wrong—it was about choosing to listen, to forgive, and to reach across invisible walls with kindness.

Retirement After Being Alone: Mr. Uday's Journey of Rediscovery

One powerful takeaway from Mr. Uday's journey is the profound impact of feeling truly understood. For a long time, he believed that nobody saw his pain, his grief, or the emotional storm he was weathering. In trying to control everything around him, he was silently crying out, *"Somebody understands me."* It wasn't until his granddaughter Riya saw him not just as a grandfather but as a person with emotions, memories, and unspoken needs that something changed. Through her simple gesture—a drawing filled with love and memory—she told him without words, *"Somebody understands you."* That moment sparked a transformation. It reminds us that even the smallest acts of empathy can be life-changing. Sometimes, all it takes is one person to make us feel seen, heard, and valued—and from there, healing begins.